CLOSER *to* NOWHERE

ALSO BY ELLEN HOPKINS

Crank

Burned

Impulse

Glass

Identical

Tricks

Fallout

Perfect

Tilt

Smoke

Traffick

Rumble

The You I've Never Known

People Kill People

CLOSER *to* NOWHERE

ELLEN HOPKINS

G. P. PUTNAM'S SONS

G. P. PUTNAM'S SONS

An imprint of Penguin Random House LLC, New York

G. P. Putnam's Sons is a registered trademark of Penguin Random House LLC.

Visit us online at penguinrandomhouse.com

Library of Congress Cataloging-in-Publication Data
Names: Hopkins, Ellen, author.
Title: Closer to nowhere / Ellen Hopkins.
Description: New York: G. P. Putnam's Sons, [2020] | Summary: Told in two voices, sixth-grade
cousins Hannah and Cal learn a lot about family when circumstances throw them together under
one roof and Hannah's love of order clashes with Cal's chaotic behavior.
Identifiers: LCCN 2020017670 (print) | LCCN 2020017671 (ebook) |
ISBN 9780593108611 (hardcover) | ISBN 9780593108628 (ebook)
Subjects: CYAC: Novels in verse. | Family life—Fiction. | Emotional problems—Fiction. |
Cousins—Fiction.
Classification: LCC PZ7.5.H67 Clo 2020 (print) | LCC PZ7.5.H67 (ebook) | DDC [Fic]—dc23
LC record available at https://lccn.loc.gov/2020017670
LC ebook record available at https://lccn.loc.gov/2020017671

Printed in the United States of America
ISBN 9780593108611

1   3   5   7   9   10   8   6   4   2

Design by Eileen Savage | Text set in Maxime Std and Avenir

This book is dedicated to every kid who struggles to fit in. Each of you is unique, with your own special gifts and challenges. Share your gifts. Conquer your challenges. Walk proudly. Shine your light. The world is a better place because you're in it.

FACT OR FICTION:
You Can Know Where You Are and Still Be Lost

Answer: Take it from me.

I'm Cal, and I've been lost
since Mom died three years ago.

Oh, I could show you exactly
where this town is on a map,
lead you through the maze
of its streets, though I've only
lived here fourteen months,
three weeks and
two days.

I'm safe for now.
But I don't know
how long that will last.

I'm afraid
if I start to believe
I belong here,
everything
will change
again.

It's like off in the distance
I can see something
that could be home,
but every time I start
in that direction
it's farther away.

And no matter how hard
I try to reach it,
I only get closer
to nowhere.

Definition of *Hannah Lincoln*:

Wait a second.
You want *me* to define me?
Let me think.
Okay, here goes.

I'm Hannah Lincoln.
Dad says we're not related
to the dead president
and I believe him.
I don't look anything like
Honest Abe.

He was tall and skinny.
I'm short and built muscly like
a gymnast, because I am one.

He had dark hair.
Mine's red, with highlights,
like the color of a new penny.

He had a beard.
Um, no. Not even
a hint of hair on my chin.

But I am like President Lincoln
in a good way. One time,
my dad told me I was

Honest as the day is long.

When I said I didn't know
what that meant, he said,

> *Trustworthy, twenty-four*
> *hours every day.*

I asked because I need to
understand what stuff means
and how things work.

If I don't get what someone
says, I'll make them explain.

If I don't know the definition
of a word, I'll look it up.

If I don't get the hang of a gymnastics
move, I'll practice until I nail it.

That's important because
I've got a giant dream.
Which doesn't make me
a dreamer. I'm a doer.

Focused.
Dedicated.
Not afraid to work hard.

My coach would tell you
I'm all of those things,
and that they're exactly what
it will take to qualify
for the Olympics one day.

Well, those, plus tons
of help from my family.
I used to count on that.

My parents were my support
system. Totally solid.
We were a great team.

But, like, three years ago,
just before I turned nine,
Mom's sister got leukemia
and died. And everything
started to fall apart.

Definition of *Status Quo*:
The Way Things Are [Were]

Three years ago,
this was the way
things were.

We lived
(still do)
in a nice house
in a sweet neighborhood
in a small San Diego suburb.

Dad was
(still is)
a computer whiz,
building systems
all around Southern California.
He had dinner with us
pretty much every night.

Mom was
(still is)
the person who made
me love dance.
She worked at a studio,
teaching jazz and ballet
to help pay for my own lessons.

I went
(still do)
to a grade school just around
the corner from home.

I'd taken dance for five years
and been in gymnastics for four.
My parents came to every recital,
cheered for me at every meet.
They sat close. Held hands.

I was okay being an only child.

Today, this
is our status quo.

Mom quit her job
to take care of Aunt Caryn
when she got sick and needed
a bone marrow transplant.
She never went back
to work. I wish she would.
I think she was happier.

I know Dad was.

He has to work twice
as hard now. He travels
around the country, showing
other people how to build
computer systems.
We eat too many dinners
without him.

But when he's home,
he and Mom argue a lot.
Mostly about money and bills.
I hate when they yell.

I'm in Mrs. Peabody's sixth-
grade class, at the same school
I've gone to since kindergarten.
I still do dance and gymnastics.
Mom drives me to every recital
and meet. Dad misses some.
When he's there, they sit
with a space between them.

Oh, and now I'm sharing
everything—home, parents,
even my teacher—with my cousin.
I'm not so okay with that.

Definition of *Resent*:
Feel Bothered By

Cal moved in
a little more than a year ago.
He wasn't exactly a stranger.

Aunt Caryn was his mom,
and she and my mom were more
than sisters. They were identical twins.

> *Two halves of a whole,*
> Mom called them.

They were close, but they
didn't live near each other.
Aunt Caryn moved to Arizona
before Cal was born.

She visited once in a while
and came to a couple of family
reunions. Talk about trouble!

I guess when Aunt Caryn met
Cal's dad and dropped out
of college, it made Grandma mad.

> *They hardly talk at all anymore,*
> Mom told me once. *And when*
> *they do, they end up shouting.*

"So why does Aunt Caryn
go to the reunions?" I asked.
"Grandma's always there."

Caryn still wants to be part
of the family, and she wants
Cal to know his relatives.

"I think Grandma should
forgive her," I said.

I think so, too. But my mother
has a hard time with forgiveness.
She thinks it's a sign of weakness.

Grandma still hadn't forgiven
her when Aunt Caryn died.

I'll never forget that day.
Mom cried and cried.
When she finally stopped,
her face was so puffed up,
I could barely see her eyes.

I lost a piece of myself, she said.

Maybe Cal living with us
is like getting that piece back.

Maybe that's why Mom lets him
get away with everything,
from pranks to meltdowns to lies.
I'm sorry, but I resent that.

> *Try to find a little sympathy,*
> Mom urges. *After Caryn passed,*
> *things got pretty rough for Cal.*

His dad took him after
the funeral, but the details
of the next two years are a mystery.
And no one's giving out clues.

> *You'll have to wait for Cal to tell*
> *you,* Mom says. *It's not up to me.*

Whatever happened, I feel sorry
for Cal. If my mom died, I'd be lost.
Cal must feel lost sometimes, too.
So, yeah, I want to forgive his quirks.

Definition of *Quirk*:
Weird Habit

Still, Cal isn't easy to live
with. I like order. Routine.
He's the king of chaos.

Our spare room is Cal's lair
now. Mom let him paint it
charcoal and doesn't even
yell about the mess—
greasy wrappers here,
dirty clothes there.
Imagine what's crawling
around in his closet!

Gross.

I have to share a bathroom
with him, which might not
be so bad, except he forgets
to drop the toilet seat.
I've splashed down
in the dark
more than once.

Gross squared.

Cal drinks milk straight
from the carton,
and brushes his teeth
without toothpaste.
Sometimes he doesn't
brush them at all.

Gross cubed.

Those are little things.

But Cal has bigger problems.
Like right now at school,
we're outside for recess.

It never gets really cold here,
but it's early November. The sky
is gray and the air is kind of sharp.
Almost everyone is playing ball.

       Softball.
           Kickball.
                Tetherball.
                   Basketball.

But Cal is sitting against
a wall of the sixth-grade
building, face in a book.
He reads, like, three a week.

Our teacher, Mrs. Peabody,
keeps telling him to slow down.

       Comprehension means more
       than word count, she says.

But, no. He *has* to read more
than anyone else, and asks
for books that are *long* and
advanced. Sometimes it seems
like he's showing off.

The problem with that
is it can draw the attention
of bullies, especially those
who think it's hilarious
to make someone freak out.

There go two now,
and they're headed
in Cal's direction.

This could be bad.

Definition of *Intervene*:
Get Involved

> Vic Malloy is
>> taller than average
>> square
>> buzz-cut
>> meaner than snot.

> Bradley Jones is
>> a head shorter
>> round
>> faux-hawked
>> meaner than snot.

They close in on Cal.
I know what they've got in mind.
Cal's been in this school
for a year. They've seen
him melt down before.

I nudge my best friend
Misty, who's watching
the tetherball wind
and unwind around the pole.

"Look."

> *Uh-oh*, she says.

We're all the way across
the field, so we can't hear
what the boys are saying.
But when Cal looks up,
his expression is easy to read.

Annoyed.

Anxious.

Angry.

Think we should intervene?
Misty asks. *Like the counselor
told us to do in that assembly?*

"Yeah. We probably should."

But before we can, Vic kicks
the book, and when it goes
flying, Cal jumps to his feet.
The other boys laugh
and move in toward him.

Some kids might respond
by raising their fists.
Others might shrink back
against the wall.

Cal screams.
Like a siren.

                    Piercing.
              Panicky.
        Painful.

Everyone stops
what they're doing.
Turns to stare.

The playground-duty
teachers go running.

Vic and Bradley
slink off into the shadows.
Laughing hysterically.

              And Cal
              is still screaming.

Definition of *Mortified*:
Totally Embarrassed

Our principal, Mr. Love
(yeah, I know), comes
to see what the problem is.

He puts an arm around
Cal's shoulders, steers
him toward the office.

> *Well, that was special,*
> says Misty. *Your cousin*
> *is weird, you know.*

My cheeks were already
hot. Now they're on fire.
"Hey, it's not *my* fault."

> Misty sniffs. *I didn't say*
> *it was your fault.*
> *No one thinks that.*

"So why is everyone looking
at me? I'm mortified!"

> *Hannah, you're the most*
> *popular girl in the sixth grade.*
> *Don't even worry about it.*

"Okay, fine." But my face
is still burning when the bell
rings and we go back inside.

Luckily, Cal isn't here.
Mr. Love has him working
in the office, where it's quiet.

That's an "accommodation"
of Cal's IEP. That means
Individualized Education Program.

Kids who have a hard time
learning get accommodations. It doesn't
mean they're not smart.

Cal is, for sure. But when
he has a meltdown like that one,
he can't pay attention in class.

Neither can anyone else.
Especially not me. Mom
swears Cal can't control it.

> *His therapist says when*
> *too much comes at him*
> *at once, his brain crashes.*

Crashing brain!
                  Siren screaming!
                                    Sometimes he throws things.

I get that it's not all his fault.
No one wants to be pushed
aside and made fun of.

I wish I knew how to help
him. I wish I could figure
out how to be his friend.

But that's hard
because I'm not exactly
sure who he really is.

Definition of *Disguise*:
Hide; Mask

See, Calvin Pace

is a fake kid.

Oh, he isn't like a

robot or
a cyborg
or a mannequin.

He doesn't

run
on
batteries,

and you don't have to

plug him
in to charge
him up.

Nope. Cal is

flesh and
blood
and bones,

freckled skin,

curly red hair,
and I guess
he's pretty much human.

But what you see

on the outside
is like a shell
he hides behind.

Something he built

> to disguise
> the person
> who lives inside.

Who's the real Cal?

> Sometimes I wonder.

FACT OR FICTION:
My Full Name's Calvin Lee Pace

Answer: Everyone knows that's a fact.

The questions get tougher
from here, and answering them
is painful. Which is why
I invent fictional responses.

Or say nothing.

Guys like Vic and Bradley think
they bother me, but I've lived
through some awful stuff.
Growing up with a dad like mine,
I'm lucky to be all in one piece.
Only my brain is broken.

I don't talk about that.

Instead, I read. Books quiet
the noise inside my head.
I'm like a rubber band,
mostly loose. But once in
a while I get stretched too tight,
like all the way to breaking.

I hate when I snap.

I try to hold the anger in,
but when it's trapped inside
too long, it all rushes out.
Raging. Screeching. Erupting.
Sometimes I can smell it coming.
It stinks like cigarettes.

It has to escape.

When I blow, at first it feels
great, like how a giant fart
makes your stomachache
go away. All that pressure,
pfft! But then I see how
it just looks like I'm crazy.

I know I need help then.

I glance over at Mr. Love,
who's at his desk. He's decent.
The principal at my last school
had no patience for "peculiarities."
That's what he called my weirdness.
He also said I was a pain.

And, at least once, a freak.

I guess I should be used
to that by now. But when
a kid spits a mean name,
it's like a fly buzzing around.
Mostly annoying. When an adult,
especially one who's supposed
to help, spits one my way?

Stings like a scorpion.

FACT OR FICTION:
I've Been Stung by a Scorpion

Answer: Yep, true.

I grew up in Arizona,
where scorpions
were regular visitors.

Not only to our little backyard,
but also, from time to time,
they hitchhiked inside,
attached to a shoe or pant leg.

If you research Arizona
scorpions, you'll find four
main types. None are deadly,
unless you're really old,
already sick, or a baby.

Or you might be allergic.
I'm not. But that doesn't mean
their stings didn't welt up
and throb like crazy.
Mom had a cure.

> *Baking soda paste*
> *will fix it for you.*

Baking soda, moistened
and applied like a bandage.
Which, by the way, is a poultice.
Mom made me look up the word.
She wanted me to know stuff.

I know her poultice worked.

Now I'm thinking about Mom.
I try really hard not to,
but she pops into my head
at the strangest times,
like along with scorpions.
I miss her so much.

I had her for nine years.
She's been gone three.
Today, Mom's still three-fourths
of my life. Ten years from now . . .

Will I even remember
her heart-shaped face
or that her eyes
reminded me of amber?

Will I forget how her hair
smelled like coconut
and her skin smelled like rain
when I sat on her lap?

How long until
these memories fade
to nothing?

I push all that away, go
back to my assignment:
Write a Happy Memory.

Interesting timing.

I'm not going to write
about amber eyes
or poultices.

Those memories are personal.
All mine, and nobody else's.
So I guess I'll just make
something up.

I'm finishing my totally
fictional story when the school
counselor sticks her head
through the door.

>   *Heard you had a little*
>   *trouble today.*

I shrug. "Nothing major."

>   *Let's discuss it anyway.*
>   *Bring your stuff and come on.*

I don't really mind talking
to Ms. Crowell as long as
I get to pick the subject.
I wave goodbye to Mr. Love,
follow Ms. C to her office.

FACT OR FICTION:
I Know Show Tunes

Answer: Keep reading.

Ms. C plops down in her rocking
chair, motions for me to sit
on the beanbag and give her
the lowdown on what happened
outside. It doesn't take long.

> *Okay, that was uncalled-for.*
> *I'll talk to Vic and Bradley.*
> *But what about your response?*
> *Do you think it was an overreaction?*

Sure. Sure. Blame the victim.
"I try not to react at all, but
when it feels like I'm cornered,
I need to protect myself."

> *Question: What could*
> *you have done differently?*

It's a worn-out question, and
I have to fight a hot flush
of anger, find something like
a sense of humor. "Let me think.
Oh, I know. Sing a show tune?"

> *Ms. C smiles. Do you know*
> *any show tunes, Cal?*

I hum a few lines of "Tomorrow"
from *Annie*, then move into "Ease
on Down the Road" from *The Wiz*.

Her grin grows. *I'm impressed.*
I take it you like musicals?

"My mom loved them, so
we watched them together.
She liked all kinds of movies.
Everything from Walt Disney
to Alfred Hitchcock."

Now her eyes go wide.
She let you watch Hitchcock?

"Some of them. She made me
close my eyes in the scary
parts, but sometimes I peeked."

Brave boy. She pauses, then
changes the subject. *And how
are things going at home now?*

"Okay. Uncle Bruce is gone
a lot. He travels for work.
Aunt Taryn is kind of stressed.
And Hannah is Hannah."

Are the two of you getting along?
I know it was a big adjustment.

"I don't think Hannah likes
me being around. She's used
to having things her way.
Mostly, she just ignores me."

She smiles. *Except when you*
slip a frog into her cereal?

My turn to grin. "Yeah. I guess
that was kind of hard to ignore."
I thought she was going to puke.

You've lived there for a little
more than a year. Wasn't it
supposed to be a trial period?

I nod. "The judge told us after
twelve months we could make it
permanent, but we'd all have to
agree." That includes my dad.

Pretty sure he's still in prison.
I hope so.
That's where he belongs.
I never want to see him again.
He scares me.

This time he got locked up
for armed robbery.
That means he used a gun
to steal money.
When the judge sent him away,
the deal was I'd go live with Aunt Taryn.

Temporarily.
As in, things could change.
That worries me.

But the judge also said, considering
the not-so-great way Dad took
care of me, what I want will
carry more weight. That's good.

Because the last time I heard
from Dad was on a speakerphone
in that courtroom.

> *Don't worry, son*, he said.
> *I'll come get you the minute
> they let me out of this place.*

And that is
my worst nightmare.

FACT OR FICTION:
I Once Lived in a Cave

Answer: Anything's possible.

Ms. C sends me back to class,
and when I get there,
Mrs. Peabody's voice is gentle.

> *Go on and take your seat.*
> *We're sharing the stories*
> *we wrote this morning.*

We hear about birthday
parties, puppies, and trips
to Disneyland and the zoo.

Misty's Grand Canyon one
is pretty good, but Hannah wrote
about her lame dance recital.

Guess happy memories
are boring. These people need
to get more creative.

Mrs. Peabody calls on me,
and when I stand to read,
every head swings my way.

Okay by me. I worked hard
on this story. It's more
interesting than ballet:

"When I was five, my parents
took me camping. We put up
a tent, unrolled sleeping bags.
Gathered wood for the fire.

"That night, we roasted hot dogs
on sticks and scorched
marshmallows for s'mores.
Camp food is awesome,
even when you burn it.

"After that, Mom made us play
charades, category 'fairy tales.'
I picked 'Jack and the Beanstalk.'
Dad chose 'Red Riding Hood.'
Mom went last, with 'Hansel
and Gretel.' I guess she was
hinting at something."

See how I slipped them a clue?
That's called foreshadowing.

"Next morning, I was scared to go
to the bathroom alone, but Mom
told me not to worry about the stinky
outhouses, to just go in the woods.
She gave me leftover graham crackers,
said to leave a trail of crumbs to find
my way back. And I fell for it!

"I didn't go far, but when I turned
around, everything looked the same.
Good thing I had a way to figure out
my reverse trip. Except, something
had scarfed the crumbs. I could hear
it was big, and it was crashing
through the woods, straight at me!"

They're on the edge of their seats.
Right where I want them.

"Okay, I freaked. Wouldn't you?
I ran and ran, deep into the forest.
The trees were thick, and the sun
had a hard time cutting through,
so it got darker and darker. I lost
whatever was chasing me, but
then I was lost, too. I wandered
for hours. It started to get cold.

"Luck was with me. I found a cave.
It looked empty, so I went inside.
I figured my parents were searching
and would find me anytime. Wrong!
You know who found me? A mama
grizzly and her twins. I was sure
they'd eat me. But Ma Griz knew
I was just a dumb kid in trouble.

"She let me stay. Bruno and Bella
showed me where the stream was
and taught me to find berries,
dig for termites and steal honey
from hives. It was a pretty good life
for a couple of years. I know I should've
started kindergarten sooner, but—"

> Cal . . . warns Mrs. Peabody. *This
> is supposed to be autobiographical,
> not a riff on a fairy tale.*

"It happened," I insist.

> *Calvin Pace!* huffs Hannah.
> *You were* not *raised by grizzlies!*

"Like you'd know. Why do you think
my favorite teams are from Chicago?"

> *I don't get it.*

The only "sports" Hannah gets
are gymnastics and dance.
But Mrs. Peabody understands.

> *He's talking about the Cubs
> and the Bears, Chicago's baseball
> and football teams.*

If Hannah rolled her eyes
any harder, they'd pop
right out of their sockets.
Sometimes she's just so serious!

Well, she might not be
laughing, but other kids are.
And so is Mrs. Peabody.
Guess a few people
think I'm funny.

Definition of *Punch Line*:
The End of a Joke

Cal's stupid stories
always have punch lines
attached. Usually they land
with a thud. In the really old
movies my mom likes
to watch, a trombone
or whatever would go

> waaaagh-
>   waaaagh-
>   waaaagh-
>   waaaagh.

A few kids snicker
in the way that says Cal
should just jump off a cliff.
But some of the others
actually think he's entertaining.

Misty isn't amused,
but our other best friend,
Brylee, is. I poke her.

"Don't laugh at him."

> *Why not? He's funny.*

"He's ridiculous."

> When she scowls, her nose
> wrinkles. *That's mean.*

It was, kind of, I guess.
But also true.
Still, I zip my lips.
I don't want my friends
to think I'm mean.

———

That silly story is on my mind
for the rest of the day.
It bugs me until dinnertime.
Not even the promise of lasagna
can make it go away.

Cal doesn't notice. *Man, that
smells good! Just like my mom's.*

Mom nods. *It's an old family
recipe. Our mother taught us
how to make it, but it takes most
of the day, so I don't do it often.*

Why didn't I know that?
Now I'm even more annoyed.

"Did 'Ma Griz' make termite
lasagna?" I laugh at my own
joke, and when Mom looks
confused, I explain.

That's so inventive, Cal!
You know, some people get
paid to make up stories.

He grins and reaches for
the Parmesan. *You think I could*
be an author someday?

If you work hard, you can do
anything you put your mind to.

Where have I heard that
before? Mom is a total
cheerleader. Dad can be,
too, but . . . That reminds me.

I've got a big meet in the morning.
In gymnastics there are levels
requiring more and more advanced
skills. Level one is easiest, level
ten the hardest before "elite."

Right now, I'm level eight,
and if I score well tomorrow,
I could move to nine.
I really want my dad to be there.
I hate when he misses Friday
night dinners because
I can't be sure he'll be at
my Saturday events.

"Hey, Mom. Think Dad will
make it back in time?"

> Her attention shifts to me.
> *He's sure going to try, honey.*
> *He'll catch an early flight and come*
> *straight from the airport.*
> *If there are any delays, he'll call.*

Dad's out of town for work.
He tries to get home every weekend,
but sometimes his projects go longer.

That used to mean Mom and I
would do girl stuff, like manicures.
Not anymore! Cal got into polish
one time. He didn't paint his nails.
But he did decorate the bathroom mirror.
With Red Cherry skulls and crossbones.

> Speaking of red, Cal drools
> lasagna sauce when he asks,
> *Makes it in time for what?*

"My meet."

> A giant sigh escapes him.
> *Another one? Tomorrow?*

Definition of *Impatient*:
Hannah, When It Comes to Cal

Cal knows when my meets are.
And what days I go to practice.

Almost always he has to tag along.
Cal needs supervision.

Be quiet! I say silently to myself.
Too bad myself won't listen.

"Don't be rude. Yes, another one,
and this one is really important."

>He squirms a little in his chair.
>*I thought they all were important.*

I really don't feel like explaining,
so I'm glad when Mom jumps in.

>*If Hannah does well tomorrow,*
>*she can move up a level.*

I've been working extra hard
on super difficult routines.

Not world-championship level.
Not yet. But I want to qualify one day.

The Olympics have been my dream
since the first time I watched them on TV.

I'm not sure Mom believes I'll make
it, but she gets me to every practice.

Plus every lesson, recital, rehearsal
and meet. She says she's my chauffeur.

Dad says he's my biggest fan.
I cross my fingers he'll be there.

Misty says superstitions are for people
who don't know better. She's right.

Still, what can it hurt to maybe
have a little extra luck on your side?

Dad never used to miss my competitions,
let alone random birthdays or holidays.

Sometimes he does now. He always
apologizes and means it, but . . .

I gave up on Fourth of July picnics
and Easter egg hunts a long time ago.

But when I turned eleven, my party was two
weeks late so he could be there.

Patience isn't my best thing, but I waited.
For Dad.

Definition of *Zombie*:
One of the Living Dead

I think about Dad
as I take a before-bed shower.

I know he has
      to work
      to pay the bills
      not to mention for my
                training
                gear
                and costumes.

      One time he joked, *Who
      knew tiaras were so pricey?*

"Even though I hardly ever
wear one," I answered,
and we all laughed together.
That doesn't happen
so much anymore.

I wish we could be
like we were before.

When
      each day was routine
and
      life had a solid rhythm.

When
        everything was easier
and
        all of us were happier.

After Aunt Caryn died,
Mom went blank like a zombie.
Every little bit of happiness
drained right out of her.

Definition of *Disruption*:
Trouble

Little by little, Mom got
her smile back,
but she still hasn't found
the desire to teach dance again.

Dad says she's too fragile.

I want my strong mom back.

Maybe he could be home more.

Of course, Cal would still be here.

One of the worst arguments
I've ever heard my parents
have was over Cal moving in.

> Dad was not thrilled.
> *I don't think it's a good idea,*
> *Taryn. The boy's disruptive.*

> But Mom said there wasn't
> another choice. *He's my nephew,*
> *Bruce. It's here or foster care,*
> *and I won't let that happen.*

> *I promised my sister he'd be okay.*
> *I never broke promises when*
> *she was alive. I won't start now.*

After that, they said a few
words about Cal's father,
but when they noticed me
eavesdropping, they went silent
for most of the day.

I wonder if Dad stays away
more now so he doesn't have
to deal with the disruption.

Definition of *Desperate*:
Frantic; Hopeless

I turn off the shower,
grab a towel, and as I'm drying
myself, there's a loud knock
on the bathroom door.

> *Save some hot water, okay?*

"I always do," I yell back
at Cal. "*I'm* not the rude one."

Except I kind of am
when I slowly put on
my pj's, brush my teeth
and comb my hair.

When I finally open
the door, Cal is hovering
right there outside it.

"Are you, like, stalking me?"

> *Uh, no. I'm, like, waiting*
> *for my turn in the bathroom.*
> *Good thing I'm not desperate.*

I know he means "not
desperate to use the toilet,"
but I pretend I don't.

"You are totally 'desperate.'"
He knows I'm using the funny
"no hope for you" definition.

So why does he look smacked
down? And why, as Mom
tucks me in, do I feel happy
about that? That bothers me.
Maybe I am a little mean.

FACT OR FICTION:
I Went Without a Toilet for Two Weeks

Answer: Fact, unless you count peeing
in alleys and sneaking into fast-food
places to do number two.

But that isn't something
I talk about. In fact, only
one person knows it's true,
and with luck (fingers crossed),
I'll never see him again.

One thing's for sure.
I learned how to hold it.
So waiting for Hannah is
no big deal, except I get
she's procrastinating.

That means "dawdling,"
as Mrs. Peabody might say.
Taking her own sweet time.

She thinks

it's funny

and

I deserve it.

She thinks

it bothers me.

What she doesn't get is,
even if I have to wait
a few extra minutes,

I'm sure a toilet, and
a private one,
will be available soon.

Even better is the smell
of the leftover steam
from Hannah's shower.

You can't understand
how happy shampoo
and soap will make you
until you don't have
them for a few days.

> Simple pleasures, Mom
> used to say. Don't ever
> take them for granted.

I had no clue what
she meant then, but
as I step beneath
a stream of hot water
and lather up, I totally do.

More simple pleasures:

Good books.
       Soft beds.
              Warm blankets.
                     Clean clothes.
                            Shoes that fit.
I have all of those here.

This house is filled with
simple pleasures.
So why are the people
who live in it so miserable?

FACT OR FICTION:
All Nightmares Happen at Night

Answer: Not even close.

You never know
when you might
wind up in a nightmare.

Sometimes you can find
yourself wading through one
when you're wide-awake.
I'm an expert on those.

Other times, you jump
out of sleep,
certain you just
left a bad one.

Like now.

I lie in bed

       panting
       sweating
       heart sprinting.

Like I always do,
I try to remember
exactly what made me
feel this way—

       frantic
       panicked
       terrified

—but I can't tap back
into that world.

All I know is,
I've been here before.
I can hear Mom say,
   Take it easy, Cal.
   It was only a dream.
   Breathe in. Breathe out.

What *that* tells me is,
nightmares were regular
visitors before Mom died.
I knew that, of course.

Both kinds:

   sleeping
and
   waking.

I think the awake ones
might be finished now,
though I'm afraid
to believe that's true.

But the ones that shake
me out of sleep? I doubt
those will ever desert me.

I'm guessing
they're
a regular
function
of my
malfunctioning
brain.

FACT OR FICTION:
An Owl Lives Outside My Window

Answer: Maybe yes, maybe no.

I'm not sure where it lives,
but there's an owl hoo-hooting
in a tree just beyond the glass.
It isn't the first time
the bird has come to say hello.

> The trick
> to knowing
> it's there
> is, you have
> to be awake
> before dawn.

That seems to be his favorite
time of the day to visit—just
as the darkness begins to fade
toward the gray light of morning.
Is he looking for a mate? Or for me?

> He sounds
> sad, like he
> lost something
> important
> and needs
> to find it.

I hope he does. Sometimes when
you lose things, you can't ever
get them back. I slip out of bed,
go to the window, try to catch
a glimpse of my unhappy friend.

> Weird, to label
> a random bird
> "friend." But in
> the year since
> I moved here,
> I haven't made
> another one.

Who cares? It might be nice
to have one, but it isn't really
a necessity. I'm used to being
a loner, and whenever I count
on someone else, they let me down.

> I stare hard,
> eyes fighting
> the charcoal
> color of the sky,
> and finally
> locate my owl.

He's perched on a naked branch
of a gigantic old tree, still crying.
"It's okay, buddy," I tell him.
"You'll find what you're looking for."

His head turns
right toward me,
and he hoo-hoots
before spreading
a sprawl of wings
and lifting off.

Wow. I think he heard me.

FACT OR FICTION:
Owls Are Bad Luck

Answer: I don't believe in luck.

Yeah, okay, I cross
my fingers sometimes,
mostly because
doesn't everyone?
That's habit, not superstition.

But I don't go looking
for four-leaf clovers.

I think black cats
are just as crazy
as other-colored cats.

I don't wish on stars.
Or planets. Or whatever.

> *Luck is mostly a matter*
> *of effort,* Mom told me once.

I'm not sure that's true.
I remember her trying
real hard. But she never
managed to get lucky.

Anyway, one time I told
Hannah about the owl.

An owl? Seriously?
They're bad luck, you know.

I looked it up. In some
cultures, owls are considered
messengers of death.

Like, if they visit,
someone might die.

But in other places,
they're symbols of wisdom.
And in the Harry Potter world
of wizarding, they are faithful
servants and masterful spies.

When I mentioned that to Hannah,
who's a huge HP fan (one of the few
things we have in common), it made
her mad. Don't ask me why.

But those are pretend
owls, not real ones,
she huffed, face all red.

"Superstitions aren't real,
either. My owl has been coming
around for a while now,
and everyone's still alive."

For now, you mean.
It could happen anytime.

Her eyes got all big, like
she shouldn't have said that.
But she was right.

One day someone's here.
The next day, they're gone.
And you can't have them back.

I know from experience.

FACT OR FICTION:
Kids Need Nine Hours of Sleep

Answer: Most do, according to experts.

But not me. Designated bedtime
is nine p.m. My body clock disagrees,
so Aunt Taryn lets me read
for thirty minutes under the covers.

After that, lights out.

Still, my brain has a hard time
closing down, so I usually lie
there longer before dropping off.
Then, just like this morning,
around five a.m., thoughts
start ping-ponging in my head.
Should I wear shorts? Jeans?
Isn't it awesome to have the choice?

What if everything changes tomorrow?

I get seven hours, if I'm lucky.
It seems to be plenty,
although some days I'm mad
at the world and the only
reason for that I can figure
out is maybe I'm tired.

I think that's called cause and effect.

Now, Hannah needs those nine
hours, and as far as I can tell,
she usually gets them.
Except she's always up early
before a competition.
Anxious about what's ahead.

Worry is an alarm clock.

I can hear her nervous humming
down the hall, on the way
to the kitchen. She likes to "fuel
up," as she calls it, well ahead
of her Saturday meets.

       Gotta give it time to digest.

That's what she told me, and I
think that means so she doesn't
fart mid-roundoff or -handspring.
Not sure the judges could dock her,
but it might leave a bad impression.

I'd laugh like crazy, but that's me.

It doesn't take long for her
to finish her "complex carbs"
breakfast. Energy foods, she claims.

By the time I'm dressed and
my hair's mostly pushed into place,
she's headed back to her room.

On the return trip, singing loudly.

Guess her vocal cords
have been energized.
That proves to be the case
when a scream rises
in her bedroom next door.

Mom! Seriously? Mom!

Uh-oh.

Definition of *Rad*:
Radical; Awesome

I was up in plenty of time.
Had my yogurt, fruit and cereal.
Came back to my room to get
dressed and pack my gear.

But my competition leotard
seems to be missing. I dig
through my dresser, looking
for a hint of sparkly purple.
That's our team color, which
is rad because it's my favorite.

Misty says it goes with my skin
tone and makes the copper
highlights in my hair pop.
Misty's kind of an expert.

She reads teen magazines
and always takes those tests,
                    like

> **What the Flower You Like Best
> Says About Your Personality**

          or

> **What Breed of Dog Is Most
> Compatible with Your Birth Sign.**

Misty rocks.

Hmm. Where's that leotard?
Oh, here it is, in the wrong drawer.
Why is it with my jeans?

Whatever. At least I found it.

Slip my right foot through the leg
hole. Left foot . . . Hey. It won't go.
I slide the first leg back out,
hold up the leotard. No way!

"Mom! Seriously? Mom!"

> Her footsteps come pounding
> up the hall. *What is it? Are you hurt?*

"No, but my leotard is.
Did you wash this *hot?*"

> *Of course not. If there's one thing
> I know how to do, it's laundry.*

I stretch the material this way
and that, but a three-year-old
could barely fit into this thing.

A disaster like this doesn't
just happen. Yeah, it could
have been an accident, but
I know in my heart it was—"Cal!"

> *No, Hannah. He wouldn't.
> I mean, he couldn't . . .*

There she goes, sticking up
for him again! Like he never
pranks anyone. Especially me.
"Why is he so mean?"

> *Oh, honey. Even if he did it,*
> *he was trying to be funny.*
> *We'll get you a new competition*
> *leotard. In the meantime,*
> *wear your practice one.*

"Fine." I wipe hot tears out
of my eyes. "But Coach is going
to be mad. And I will never,
ever talk to Cal again!"

> *We'll be in the car. You'd better*
> *get a move on, or we'll be late.*

Definition of *Idiom*:
A Saying That Doesn't Mean What It Says

I hope Mom makes Cal pay
for my new competition leotard.
Three months of allowance
might cover it. Maybe.

Obviously, he doesn't get
that gymnastics team members
are supposed to wear matching
outfits at meets. Like he'd care.

Luckily, my practice leotard
is the right color, minus
the sequins and glitter.
Oh yeah, and this one fits.

I cover it up with my warm-up
suit, hustle on out to the car,
hop into the back seat, try
to pretend Cal doesn't exist.

Tough to do when he's across
the seat and turns to stare.
I look out the window but can feel
his eyes on the back of my head.

> *Nice ponytail*, he taunts.
> *Make it bounce?*

My cheeks burn. He's dying
for me to respond, but I won't.
I won't. Mom starts the engine,
backs out of the driveway.

Don't say anything. Don't say
anything. We've gone maybe three
blocks, and I fight to force
the words back into my mouth.

But finally, I can't help it.
"What did you do to my leotard?"

> *Your what?*

"You know what I'm talking
about. You shrunk it!"

> *Hannah . . .* warns Mom.

> *No, I didn't*, insists Cal.

"Yes, you did!"

> *I don't even know what a lee-tard is.*

"Le-O-tard, and yes, you do."

Do not.

"Do."

> *Enough, or I'm turning the car*
> *around and we're going home.*
> The tone of Mom's voice means
> we'd better be quiet.

Cal glares at me and I glare
back and silently mouth, *Liar.*
He shrugs and offers a lopsided
smile, and the anger inside me
burns white-hot. As Dad might say,

> *Drink a little water and steam*
> *will come out of your ears.*

Some of Dad's jokes aren't meant
to be funny. Some are just
supposed to make you think.

Definition of *Break a Leg*:
Idiom Used to Wish a Performer Good Luck

I stay mad all the way across
town, to the school where
the meet will soon begin.
Mom pulls into the parking
lot and finds a space.

> *Cal, you go on inside and save*
> *a couple of seats. I'll be right there.*

We watch him disappear
through the big doors
into the gym. "You trust him
to do that all by himself?"

> *He's not a baby, Hannah.*

"No. Just a weirdo."

> Mom turns to talk to me
> over the seat. *I understand*
> *he's not easy to get along with,*
> *but a little compassion would*
> *go a long way toward—*

"I try, Mom, you know I do."

> *Maybe try a little harder.*

Sure, I think. *Just wait*
until he starts shrinking
your *clothes*. But out loud,
I say, "Okay, Mom."

> *Great. Now, break a leg.*
> *We'll be cheering for you.*

I go on inside, find the list
of our event rotations.

First up for my squad: bars.
That's good and bad.
I can hear Dad tease,

> *Hang in there.*

Which means

> *Don't give up.*

But for me, it's got another
meaning, too, because
out of all my events,

the uneven

parallel bars

have always
been the most
challenging.

Kips
casts and
handstands

        aren't so hard, but releasing
        a bar to do a trick, then catching
        it again?

                Hit
                    or
                        miss.

So, starting with bars
is good because I can
get them out of the way.

        And bad, because if I mess up,
        my focus will be wrecked
        for the rest of the meet.

Definition of *Glamorous*:
Dazzling; Beautiful

Misty catches up to me
in the locker room.

> *Practice leotard?*
> *What's up with that?*

My jaw tightens and
I grit my teeth. "Ask Cal."

> *Oh. Is he* here? Misty knows
> he can be a distraction.

"Where else? Not like we can
leave him home alone.
He'd probably blow up
the microwave or something."

> *True. And it's not like anyone*
> *would want to babysit him.*

"Not even for a million dollars."

> *Well, that leotard looks okay.*
> *It's just not* elegant. Misty makes
> her voice all husky and low,
> like an old-time Hollywood star.

Sometimes Misty watches
ancient movies with Mom and me.

Mom thinks they're rad.

"I know it isn't *glamorous*,
but it will just have to do."

> *Come on. Let me do your makeup.*
> *Maybe some glittery eye shadow*
> *will help.* Misty knows makeup, too.

Mom only lets me wear it
for performances, so I'm
glad to have Misty's help.
If I tried to do it myself,
I'd probably look like a clown.

Shadow.
     Mascara.
          Blush.

When I look in the mirror,
I have to smile. My eyes
and leotard are color
coordinated, and there's
at least a little sparkle.

> *Better?* asks Misty.

"Better," I agree.

Which is good,
because when Coach calls
us for warm-ups, if she notices
what I'm wearing,
she doesn't say a word.

As I jog and jump around
the mat, I find Mom and Cal
in the stands, but not Dad.
Well, there's still lots of time
before the meet starts.

If he's a little late, it's better
than him not making it at all.
Especially if I flub the bars.

Definition of *Pirouette*:
Whirl; Spin

Coach claps her hands.
> *Okay, girls, line up.*
> *Time for the march in.*

My tummy flutters as we line
up by height, putting me
right in the middle of the stack.

A rhythmic applause fires up,
and the announcer declares that
the competition has officially begun.

When our team—the Comets—
is announced, we salute the judges,
then continue to the bars.

I watch my teammates perform
with one eye, keep the other
on the stands. There. There's Dad!

I give him a little wave and he blows
me a kiss, which gives me confidence.
Also, a huge attack of nerves.

I close my eyes, take deep breaths.
When my name is called, I tell
myself: *You've got this.*

> I spring onto the lower bar.
> Glide forward, backward.

Point the toes. Point the toes.

        Lift my pointed toes to the bar.
        Rotate back beneath it.

Arms straight. Arms straight.

        Arms straight, up into a handstand.
        Pirouette to face the other way.

Legs together. Legs together.

        Legs together, stand on low bar.
        Jump over to the high one.

Elbows locked. Elbows locked.

        Elbows locked, arms straight.
        Legs together. Take a giant swing.

Set up dismount. Set up dismount.

        Setting up my dismount, another swing.
        Reach for height. One twist. Down I come.

Nail the landing. Nail the landing.

        I nail the landing.
        Not even a small stumble.

The judges dock me a little
for not holding my handstand
long enough and a slight elbow break.

But I did well, and when my score
comes up a 9.6 out of
a possible 10, I hear my parents.

Cheering together.
Applauding together.
Sitting together.

Exactly the way things
should be. And together,
they're double proud of me.

Definition of *Contentment*:
The Feeling That All Is Well

Figure in Cal,
who's whooping, too,
that's a triple dose of pride.

A huge wave
of contentment
splashes over me,
and as we move to the next
event rotation, my confidence grows.

That's good, because
the four-inch-wide padded steel
balance beam is especially challenging
to tumble and dance across.

With every landing, your feet
have to hit just right so you
don't fall off the narrow beam.

Today, I ace every move
from my mount, straight
into sideways splits,
to my back-somersault dismount.

It's a near-perfect performance,
barely a bobble.

I glance up into the stands.

Dad gives me a thumbs-up.
Mom does a little happy dance.
And Cal? He's not around.
As we rotate again, this time
to the floor, I tap Misty's shoulder.
"Looks like Cal disappeared."

>   *You should be so lucky.*
>   *He can't have gone very far.*

Unfortunately, that's true.

FACT OR FICTION:
The Floor Is Hannah's Best Event

Answer: Most of the time.

I've only seen her mess up
once or twice. She's really good,
and I think it's because the floor
combines tumbling and dance.

You can tell she loves it.

That's her next rotation,
and to make up for the dumb
leotard (which I did accidentally shrink,
to be honest), I ask Aunt Taryn,

"Want me to video Hannah's
floor routine?" It's on the far
side of the gym, so shooting
it on a phone from our seats
wouldn't be as good as up close.

>   *You want her to trust you*
>   *with her cell?* asks Uncle Bruce.

>   *I think it's a nice gesture,*
>   responds Aunt Taryn.

>   *That's a brand-new phone,*
>   *and it cost a pretty penny.*

It belongs to me, Bruce.
I'll take care of it as I see fit.

These two argue a lot. I wonder
if they've always bickered,
or if it's mostly my fault.

I'm pretty sure it's me.

FACT OR FICTION:
Uncle Bruce Wasn't Happy About Me Moving In

Answer: That is a fact.

He pretends it's fine, but I know

>   *what upset looks like*
>   *what impatience sounds like*
>   *how it feels when anger comes your way.*

I can see disapproval

>   *in his eyes*
>   *in his body language*
>   *in how he avoids touching me.*

It's weird. I'm not sure if

>   *he worries he'll hurt me*
>   *he thinks I'll freak out*
>   *he believes I'm contagious.*

Doesn't matter. I'm not asking

>   *for hugs*
>   *for pats on the back*
>   *to be tucked in at night.*

But I wish he'd make me feel

>   *understood*
>   *encouraged*
>   *wanted.*

FACT OR FICTION:
All Families Are Dysfunctional

Answer: Can't speak for all of them.

I've only known two,
which is
actually one,

      broken   in half.

      The left half   The right half
      is beginning   has been ripped
      to come unraveled.   to shreds.

A pair of threads
connect
what remains.

      Aunt Taryn.   And me.

She can never be Mom.
But she comes close.

Uncle Bruce will never be Dad.
And that's a good thing.

Living with them
isn't perfect for any of us.
But what is perfect
when it comes to a family?

I wonder
if I'll ever know.

FACT OR FICTION:
Cell Phone Videography Is a Talent of Mine

Answer: Guess we'll find out.

Aunt Taryn takes a chance
and hands me her fancy phone.

> *You know how to work*
> *the camera, don't you?*

I don't have a phone of my own,
but I've watched other kids.
I locate the little camera picture
on the screen. "Push this."

Which gives me some options,
all self-explanatory.
I take a quick practice session.
Still shot first. "Smile!"

Aunt Taryn grins. Uncle Bruce
looks surprised. Captured.

"Now a quick video. Sing!"
Instead, they make silly faces.
Forever remembered through
technology. "Okay. I've got it."

> *Be careful where you stand.*
> *Don't get too close to the mat.*

"Understood. But I'd better move
or I'll miss her performance."

I hold the phone against my chest,
do my best to keep it safe.

I start down the bleacher stairs,
and as I go, I hear Uncle Bruce say,

> *Bet you a hundred dollars*
> *this doesn't turn out well.*

I'll show him! I'll take the most
amazing video of Hannah ever!
I just have to find the right
place to stand. Not too close.

But not too far. And the rotten
thing is, I'm sort of height deficient.

Which means I have to find a space
between one super tall coach
and some guy built like a bulldozer.
I move this way. That.

Hannah steps into the corner
of the mat and signals she's ready.

Her music—Imagine Dragons' "On Top
of the World"—fires up, and off she goes.
Her first tumbling run is awesome,
and I do a pretty good job of framing it.

At least, I think I do. Now she does
a few dance moves. I get those, too.

She retreats into the opposite corner,
preparing to launch her second
tumbling run, and just as she takes
off, the bulldozer dude pushes in front of me.

"Hey, man. Move."

He doesn't, so I go around him.
I'm so focused on catching the action
that I don't notice where I am.
Bam! I bump into the judges' table.

Still trying to hold on to the shot,
I don't see whoever grabs the back
of my shirt and yanks. Hard.

"Leave me alone! I'm just trying
to get a video!" Now it's ruined.
My heart races and blood throbs
hot through my veins.

You can't be here! yells the man,
who turns out to be security.

"If you can, I can!" I fight
to hold my ground, but a couple
of coaches start pushing the guy
and me toward the exit.

The competition has halted and
I notice Hannah, who's crying.

All of a sudden, Uncle Bruce appears.
He's puffing like he just finished a sprint.

He grabs hold of my arm,
tugs hard. *Let's go, Cal.*

I jerk away. "Don't touch me!"

The phone flies out of my hand, smashes
against the floor. "Look what you
did!" I shout at Uncle Bruce.

What I did? His face is the color
of overripe cherries—blotchy purple.

Take it easy, Bruce. Aunt Taryn
is cool and calm as an April breeze.

She retrieves her phone,
and pushes between the men and me.
They let go, but I stay rigid,
fists clenching and unclenching.

Aunt Taryn looks me straight
in the eye, and it could be Mom
standing there, shaking her head.
Disappointed. In me.

We should leave now.

I drop my gaze to the floor. "Okay."
Now I glance over at Hannah.
If scowls could kill, I'd be in my grave.
She's steaming. *Sorry*, I mouth.

Aunt Taryn puts an arm around
my shoulders, steers me away.

FACT OR FICTION:
The Judges Will Let Hannah Start Over

Answer: *shrug*

I chance looking back
as we start toward the exit.
Hannah's coach says something
to her. She nods, and Coach
goes over to talk to the judges.

I have no idea what the rules
are, but they have to let
her go again, don't they?
It was the security guy's
fault, not Hannah's.

Guess crying messes up
a girl's makeup, because even
from here I can see dark streaks
running down Hannah's cheeks.
When the light hits them
just right, they glitter.

Her team has gathered
around her, watching
Misty wipe Hannah's eyes
and face with a tissue.

I turn away, and as the big
door closes behind me,

I hear "On Top of the World"
start again. One good thing.
But there's plenty of bad
to get sorted out, with me
right in the middle.

Aunt Taryn directs me toward
her car, and when we get
there, she opens the front
passenger door.

> *You can sit up here. Just*
> *don't fiddle with stuff, okay?*

She knows I like to push
buttons and see what they do.
I've been a "fiddler" since
I was little. Mom told me
I learned how to use a TV
remote before I could walk.

"Whatever you say."

She starts around the car,
pauses, then says,

> *Oh, no. I left my jacket inside.*
> *Stay here. I'll be right back.*

I sit, not touching anything,
trying to quiet the noise
inside my head. It's loud.
Tiny explosions of anger
sizzle like sparklers.

It wouldn't take much
to turn them back into
a major display of fireworks.

Definition of *Runner-Up*:
Not Quite the Best; Non-Winner

So, yeah, the judges agreed
to let me start over. I tried.

But when the music began,
I'd lost my stride. The tumbling
passes were good enough,
but my dance was stiff
and I forgot to smile.

Small dings against my final
score, but enough to keep
me well out of first place.

It's so not fair.

Our last event of the rotation
is the vault. Straightforward.

> Sprint down the runway.
> Hit the springboard.
> Land hands on the vault table.
> Push off into a pike somersault.
> Stick the landing. And repeat.

I've practiced it hundreds
of times. Don't even have to
think about it. I lift an arm,
signaling I'm ready. Off I go.

Full speed down the runway.
                  But now I see my parents.
                              Not clapping. Not cheering.
                                          Arguing.

I lose
            concentration
            momentum
            velocity.

And it all goes wrong.

Not enough
                  speed
                  spring
                  straightness.

I land with a thud,
stumble backward,
just barely keep my feet.
The audience groans.

            Coach hustles over. *Hannah
            Lincoln, I want you to dig down
            deep and take control. You've
            worked too hard to give up
            like this. Do you understand?*

I nod. "Yes, Coach."

Let's see a perfect second vault.

It isn't perfect, but it's really
good. Problem is, averaged
with my first score, it still
leaves me near the bottom
of the vault leaderboard.

The girls all finish their rotations
and the judges make their final
tallies. It wasn't my best day,
but neither was it my worst.

I earn a silver medal
in balance beam,
and another in bars.
The two scores together
don't level me up, but
they do help the Comets
finish second overall
and take the runner-up trophy.

Too bad only one of my parents
is here to see me accept my awards.

Definition of *Incorrigible*:
Not Fixable

The Lincoln family tradition
is to go for pizza after every meet.
Usually, Misty comes along,
and sometimes the whole team
celebrates at Bruno's Pies.

But after that runner-up
performance, not to mention
the commotion with Cal,
everyone begs off, including Misty.

>   *But I'll see you at Brylee's party*
>   *tomorrow, right?*

"Guess so."

>   *Gee, don't sound so jazzed.*

"Sorry. Yeah, I'll be there."

Brylee's birthday blast is at
the skating rink, and all the kids
are excited because it's boy-girl.

Not that anyone in our class
is going together, and the only
reason both girls and boys
are coming is because
Brylee's mom said
everyone had to be invited.

Everyone.

Which is why I'm not exactly
thrilled, because that includes Cal.
Wonder what kind of stunt he'll pull.
The possibilities are endless.

Dad meets me at the locker room
door. He lifts me high, smooshes
me in a bear hug, and his bushy
blond mustache tickles my cheek.

> *Great meet, Bug. You were awesome!*

The nickname makes me smile.
When I was, like, three or four,
my very first dance troupe
was the Ladybugs. Dad's into
abbreviations. "I could've done better."

> *Hey, you killed the beam and
> rocked the bars, and if it wasn't for . . .
> well, you know.* He changes the subject.
> *Hope you're hungry. I called Bruno's
> and ordered an extra-large Super Combo.*

Way to erase my smile.
"Cal's coming, too?" Super Combos
are his favorite. I like them
okay, but Hawaiian is better.
Why is *he* getting the reward?

*The plan is for Mom and Cal
to meet us there. Oh, and I
also ordered a small Hawaiian.*

"All for me?"

*Who else? Let's go. I skipped
breakfast to make my plane
and I'm starving.*

We're quiet for the first
part of the ride, but finally
I say, "I'm glad you made it today."

*I give it my best try every time.
By the way, if I haven't told you
lately, I'm so proud of what
you've accomplished, I could burst!*

"Don't do that. Then you'll be
gone forever." I meant it as a joke,
but it didn't come out funny.
"I wish you could be home more."

I know. I miss you, too. He thinks
for a minute. *You should probably
know I have some big contracts
coming up and might be gone
even more for a while.*

"No!"

I'm sorry, but we need the income.

Money. Right. Or maybe
he'd rather be on the road.
Alone. Away from the problems
at home. Especially one very
big problem named Cal.

"Hey, Dad? Are you and Mom
okay?" They have to be. I'd die
if they got divorced, like Brylee's
parents. She hardly ever sees
her father. I need mine.

Before Dad can answer, his phone
buzzes and the car's hands-free
system picks up for him. It's Mom.

> *Um . . . We've had a little trouble.*
> *Can you bring the pizza home?*

Dad scowls. *What happened now?*

> *The screen on my phone is totaled.*
> *I told Cal he'll have to help pay for*
> *the repair. He insisted it was your*
> *fault, that you have to cover it, then*
> *jumped out of the car and took off.*

Not again! Dad complains.

Cal says it's how he cools off.
But he wants to make us worry.
Last time he was gone for hours.
Dad was about to call the police
when Cal wandered in. He won't say
where he goes, only that it's safe.

I'm afraid so, Mom answers.

That boy is incorrigible! You know
how my father would've handled
it? He'd have taken off his belt and—

I know, Bruce. You've mentioned
it before. But that's how Cal got
this way. I'm going to look for him.
You and Hannah have fun.

Dad rubs his right temple. *How*
can she be so patient with him?

"Good question."

But what did she mean by
that's how he got this way?

Definition of *Migraines*:
Horrible Headaches That Come Regularly

By the time we get to Bruno's,
I've quit worrying about Cal.
I don't want to think about
him at all. Not when I can
spend time alone with Dad.

Our pizzas are ready. I trade
Dad a slice of my Hawaiian
for a piece of Super Combo.
It's nice to share with him.

After we eat, we play a few
arcade games. I like the car-
racing ones. Dad prefers
"good old-fashioned pinball."

Little by little, we start to relax.
By the time we box up
our leftovers and head home,
we're both in better moods.

When we walk in the door,
Dad carrying most of an extra-
large Super Combo, the house
is silent. Mom must be here.
Her car's in the driveway.

Taryn? calls Dad.

In the kitchen.

I drop my gear bag by the door,
go to show Mom my new medals.
"I took silver in bars and beam."

I thought so. Congratulations.

Dad puts the pizza box on
the counter. *Did you find Cal?*

*No. Not a sign of him. I drove
all through the neighborhoods.
I know he says it's safe wherever
he goes, but I wish I could confirm that.*

Dad sighs. *Do you have any idea
where he might go, Bug?*

I shake my head. "Lots of kids
from school live around here,
but he doesn't have any friends.
Not that I know of, anyway."

I think about Misty and Brylee
and the others in our tight circle.
It must be sad not to have friends.
But who'd want to buddy up with Cal?

*How long do I give it before
I really start to worry?* Mom
asks that question every time.

Dinnertime, answers Dad.
He must be getting hungry.

        He is always home for dinner,
        agrees Mom, *or at least by dark.*

But Mom is anxious long
before that. She gets one
of her migraines and has to
lie down while Dad catches
up on some paperwork.

That leaves me alone to paint
my nails for Brylee's party.

Definition of *Psychedelic*:
Having an Intense Color or Swirling Pattern

I'm at the kitchen table, applying
a gloss coat, when Cal barrels in
through the back door. Yep,
it's right around dusk.

> *I'm home. Did you miss me?*

He thinks it's funny? "Where've
you been? Mom's worried sick."

> *How about you?*

"Was *I* worried? No way. You're smart
enough to use sidewalks and cross
at the lights, I think. And no one
with a brain would want to kidnap you."

> *Funny you should say that.*

He puts a piece of Super Combo
on a plate and into the microwave.
Thankfully, it doesn't blow.

> *I mean, here I am, walking down*
> *the street—okay, the sidewalk—*
> *when this old van, painted all hippie—*
> *you know, like . . . what's that word*
> *that means with swirly colors and stuff?*

"Psychedelic?" Last Halloween, Misty
and I dressed like hippies. The lady
at the thrift store where we bought
our outfits called them "psychedelic."

That's it. So, this psychedelic van
pulls up next to the curb. This lady—
man, was she pretty—asks for directions.
The microwave dings. *Hang on.*

FACT OR FICTION:
I Was Kidnapped by Hippies

Answer: Wouldn't everyone like to know?

I grab my pizza from the microwave,
take a huge bite. Hey, I'm wasting
away to nothing. No food for hours.
Still chewing, I continue my story.

"So, I went over to the van to help
the lady. As soon as I got close,
the side door opened and another girl
pulled me inside. There was a guy
driving and he hit the gas.
'Hey, man,' I said, 'what's up?'
The girl explained they needed
ransom money because their food
stamps ran out."

I sit across the table from Hannah,
munching pizza.

> You expect me to believe
> a roving band of hungry
> hippies kidnapped you?

"Yeah, but just wait. So, we drove
for maybe ten or fifteen minutes,
to a farm somewhere outside of town.
We bumped down a long dirt road
to get there—"

They didn't tie you up or
blindfold you or anything?
Hannah can't help herself.

This is fun. She's easy to annoy.

"Dude, I was in the back of the van
and couldn't see much. Besides, I was
interested in what they wanted,
so why would I try to jump?"

You weren't scared?

"I guess, a little. But it was all
so fascinating. I mean, those nice
ladies kept asking questions,
like what school do I go to,
and who are my parents,
and where do I live. Don't worry.
I faked the answers, so you're safe."

Hannah tsk-tsks. *Whatever.*

"Right. So, then the van stopped
and we got out, and these people,
I swear, live in teepees. I mean, nice
ones and all, with furniture and firepits.
But no bathrooms. You can go
number one behind a tree, but for
number two, you have to dig a hole."

Okay, Cal. So how did you get away?

"That's the best part of the story.
Remember the hippie movie
we watched with your mom? *Hair*?
Well, the getaway-driver guy
had long hair and reminded me
of the dude in the movie,
so I started humming that song.

"'Oh say, can you see my eyes?
If you can, then my hair's too short.'
They all got into it and started
doing other tunes from the movie.

"Then the one lady decided she wasn't
cut out for a life of crime and wanted
to go into musical theater. And
the other girl said she could do
singing telegrams. And the guy
said he should just drive his psychedelic
van for Uber, and—"

They just brought you back to town?

Wait for it. Wait for it.

"Yeah. But first I had to dig a hole."

Hannah's expression is priceless.
Apparently, she didn't care
much for the punch line.

Mom! Dad! she yells. *Cal's home!*

FACT OR FICTION:
When I Take Off, I'm Running Away

Answer: Maybe technically.

But not really.
Sometimes words
         mean different things
         to different people.

To me, running away
         means leaving with no
         plan to return.

To Uncle Bruce, it
         means ditching home
         without permission.

He believes I plan escapes
to make them worry, but I
don't think about them at all.

Argue or flee. Fight or flight.
I never know where I'm going,
but I'm not afraid of getting lost.

I've prowled this town
         its streets and alleys
         parks and playgrounds.

I've figured out
                    where the safe spaces are
                    which yards hold danger.

Yeah, there are
                    a few bad people out there
                    and a couple of mean dogs, too.

I steer wide around them.
Because that's what you do
when you know what could happen.

Anyway, nothing here even
comes close to some of the awful
things I've seen in other places.

Try being afraid of your dad
coming home, not knowing
how he'll walk through the door.

Happy and humming?
Mad at the world and yelling?
Crying, like he's totally crazy?

So, when Uncle Bruce scolds
me about the dangers
lurking beyond the front yard?

I sit, munching pizza, while
his lecture goes in one ear
and straight back out the other.

I guess he notices, because
he demands to know if I heard
a single word he said.

"Uh, yeah. I'm not deaf.
My problem isn't hearing.
Mrs. Peabody says it's retention."

FACT OR FICTION:
Some People Lack a Sense of Humor

Answer: One of them is staring at me right now.

Two, actually. Although
Hannah can find one
sometimes. Just not with
me attached to the joke.

Uncle Bruce, though?
I'm not sure I've ever seen
him laugh, at least not
the kind that makes you
believe he thinks something
is hilarious. Not his style.

> *So, do you want to tell*
> *us where you've been?*

Hannah beats me to it.
Apparently, he was kidnapped
by a gang of hippies who
he convinced to let him go
by singing songs from Hair.

Uncle Bruce looks skeptical,
so I start, "Give me a head
with hair . . ."

> *Cal, you've got to quit inventing*
> *these ridiculous stories.*

"Why? Aunt Taryn says
they're good practice
for being a writer."

Speaking of Aunt Taryn,
here she finally comes.
She looks sick. Her face
is chalky and she's shaking.
"Do you feel okay?" I ask her.

            Better now, thank you.

        Mom had a migraine, explains
        Hannah. *Because of you.*

                    *Now, Hannah. That's not
                    one hundred percent true.
                    Anyway, the migraine's better
                    now, so can we please move on?*

Sounds like a decent plan.
"Are you hungry?" I ask her.
"I saved you some Super Combo."

            You should eat, Taryn, says
            Uncle Bruce. *And while you do,
            we can discuss consequences.*

Oh, boy. Here it comes.
Not that I didn't expect
some kind of punishment,
but this is beginning to feel
like a spectator sport.

I mean, Hannah's sitting
there smirking, and I bet
she's got something to say.

And, oh yeah, she does.

> She clears her throat. *Well,*
> *I, for one, think he should*
> *have to miss Brylee's party.*

All the anger I stuffed
back inside threatens
to erupt again. "Well, I,
for one, wonder why
it's any of your business."

> *Maybe because you*
> *wrecked my day.*

My head tilts forward.
"I'm really sorry, Hannah."
Now I look up again, at
Aunt Taryn. "And I'm really
sorry about your phone."

But that's only part of it, Cal,
says Uncle Bruce. *Every time*
you run off, we think about
calling the police. Do you want
to end up in juvenile hall?

Duh, of course I don't, but I
think it's an empty threat.
Question is, do I give him
the answer he wants or respond
with a witty comeback?
"Private suite or double room?"

FACT OR FICTION:
Some Witty Comebacks Fall Flat

Answer: Afraid so.

Hannah wants to laugh.
I can tell. Aunt Taryn, too.
Uncle Bruce? Not so much.

> *I'm serious, Cal. You might*
> *not have thought about this,*
> *but if law enforcement gets*
> *involved, it could complicate things.*

Okay, that sounds major.
A low hum like a faraway
beehive starts up inside my head.
"Like, what kind of things?"

He doesn't answer right away,
and the buzzing grows louder.
I start to rock in my chair,
but force my voice low. "Like what?"

> He takes a deep breath.
> *Like permanent guardianship.*

That hits me hard. I jump up
from the table, knocking the chair
back into the wall. "That's what
you want. To get rid of me."

Jaw rigid, Uncle Bruce says,
*You're wrong. I don't want that
at all. Sit down and apologize.*

The noise in my brain
is so loud, it's like a billion
bumblebees. It makes me
scream. "Apologize for what?"

> *For overreacting, not to mention
> putting a ding in my wall.*

"*Your* wall. Right. How could I
forget this is *your* house?"

I stomp from the room,
slamming the door so hard,
the windows rattle.

That seems to scare the bees.
Their buzzing quiets a little.
But I'm all the way in my room
before they go back to their hive.

It takes even longer for Uncle
Bruce's words to sink in:

> *I don't want that at all.*

He said he doesn't want
to get rid of me.

I wish
I could
believe him.

Definition of *Villain*:
Bad Guy

Mom drops a half-eaten slice
of pizza on her plate, scurries
off after Cal, eyes wide and
mouth forming a stiff O.

> Dad sits down again and
> swivels toward me.
> *What just happened, Bug?*

A line from a movie Mom likes
to quote floats into my brain.
"What we've got here is
failure to communicate."

> *Exactly.* He paints on a tilted
> half smile. *From awful
> to worse in thirty seconds.
> Guess I'm the villain now.*

"Nuh-uh. Not your fault.
Anyway, you'll always
be the good guy to me."

> *Even if you're the one
> who's in trouble?*

"I'm never the one who's
in trouble." Which is only
true since Cal's been here.
But that's beside the point.

I don't know how to reach
the boy. I wish I did.

"Maybe he doesn't want
to be reached."

My thought exactly.

Mom returns and interrupts,
What was your thought exactly?

That maybe Cal resists help.

She sighs. *I don't think that's*
true, but I have a feeling
he doesn't truly believe it's available.

I try to change the subject.
"Want me to reheat your pizza?"

Thanks, but I kind of lost
my appetite. Maybe a little later.

How did you leave things
with Cal? asks Dad. *Consequences?*

We settled on some extra chores.
And no TV or gaming for a week.
Oh, and he's willing to go back
into therapy. I think we should try it.

Cal went twice a week when
he first got here. Then once a week.
When the sessions didn't change
much, he gave up on them.

What's the point? asks Dad.
He'll just tell the therapist
what he thinks she wants to hear.
He'll still run away. Still lie.

Remember what she said.
Those behaviors were how
he survived. It will take time
to convince him he's safe.

Definition of *Hyperbole*:
Exaggeration

I can't be sure, but I think
Mom is prone to hyperbole.

That's what Mrs. Peabody
said about Cal one time,
and it means he often makes
things seem more important
than they really are.

"What do you mean, how Cal
survived? Lying and melting
down kept him alive? How?"

> Look. I won't go into detail,
> but I'll give you some basics.
> You know Cal's father has been
> in trouble with the law, right?

"Yeah. He's in prison now."

> Well, this isn't the first time.
> When Cal was little—like, three
> or four—his dad started using drugs.
> The kind that make people not care
> about hurting others, including
> the people they're supposed to love.

This is giving me a bad feeling.

More than once, David got
angry and lit into Caryn.

"You mean, he *hit* Aunt Caryn?"

Mom nods. *And a few times*
Cal tried to step in between
them. David hit him, too.

"No way!" Who hits little kids?

Afraid so. And as David's addiction
got worse, so did the violence.

One night, he came home
with a stolen gun. Caryn begged
him to get rid of it. Cal was only
six and she was afraid he might
get hold of it. But David told her no.

When she insisted, he beat her
pretty badly. That was the first
time he went to prison, though
he went for armed robbery,
not assaulting his family.
He was there for two years.

Poor Aunt Caryn. And poor Cal.

When David got out, he was better
and seemed to be okay for a while.

But sometime after Caryn died,
he started doing drugs again,
and things got pretty rough for Cal.

I sort of want details.
Sort of don't.
Doesn't matter because—

Dad interrupts, *Yes, but he's safe*
here. I wish he'd quit playing
defense. I am not the enemy,
but he makes me feel like I am.

Few men in his life have ever
been kind to him, answers Mom.
That's why he resists getting close
to you. Besides, you are *sort of strict.*

What am I supposed to do?
Let the kid run all over me?

Obviously not, but—

But what? We have rules
in this house! He can't just
follow the ones he decides
are okay and ignore the rest!

"Stop! Please don't argue!
I can't stand it!"

I run to my room, flop into the chair
by my window, half of me mad at Cal
for causing more trouble, the other
half wishing I could fix all the bad
stuff that happened to him before.

Definition of *Awry*:
Wrong; Crooked

I figured Dad would come tell me
not to worry about what just went
on in the kitchen. But, no. It's Mom.

I'm still staring out the window,
watching night creep into the sky,
painting it black and blue. Like a bruise.

> Her voice is calm when she says,
> *I know it upsets you when Dad and I*
> *argue. But it's better than silence.*

I have to think about that,
but no matter how hard I try . . .
"I don't get it. What do you mean?"

> *The truth dies when no one is willing*
> *to say it out loud. Communication*
> *is vital. But your dad and I are okay.*

I want them to be great! I guess
I'll settle for okay. "Fine. But please
try to communicate without yelling."

> *Good idea. Hey, sorry I missed*
> *your last vault. Dad said it was*
> *killer. And your beam? Radical.*

I smile because I know she used
that word just for me. "Thanks.
I did all right. But I didn't level up."

> Today went awry, didn't it?
> But next time, no stopping you.
> Level nine, here you come!

"Hey, Mom? Can I ask you
something?" I was thinking
about it before she came in.

> Of course. You know you can
> ask me anything. She sits
> on the foot of my bed.

"I was just wondering.
Did . . . did Aunt Caryn
ever do drugs, too?"

> Mom hesitates, but then says,
> She experimented, but didn't like
> how they made her feel.
>
> Besides, Cal meant too much.
> She wanted to be a great mom
> and couldn't live in both worlds.

I'm glad Cal had a good mom,
since his dad wasn't so nice.
"Thanks for communicating."

Anytime. Feeling better now?
When I nod, she smiles.
Okay, then how about a movie?

"Sure." I follow Mom into
the living room, and we plop
down on the sofa together.

Let's see what we can find.
She flips through the premium
listings. *Old, new or in between?*

"I really don't care. Maybe
we should ask Dad what
he wants to watch?" Hint.

He's welcome to participate. Oh, hey.
How about this? Fantastic Beasts
and Where to Find Them.

It's a Potterverse movie, and
I'm all in. I know Harry isn't in it,
but it's supposed to be good.

"Okay! But first, let me go tell Dad."
I charge to my parents' room.
"No more paperwork. It's movie time!"

> Dad looks up, puts down
> his pen, smiles. *A movie sounds*
> *good. Okay, I'll be right there.*

That makes me happy, but on
the way back, I pass Cal's room.
He's alone with his music inside.

He was awful today—first
at my meet, and then running
away. He deserves consequences.

But he once told me Harry Potter
books got him through when
Aunt Caryn was dying. So . . .

Definition of *Morph*:
Transform; Change

I go ask Mom if we can include
Cal in our movie night.

> *Aren't you mad at him?*

"Yeah, I am. Was. Whatever.
But maybe taking away video
games is enough punishment?"

> *If you can convince your dad,
> it's okay by me. I'll go heat
> up some pizza to snack on.*

At first, I think Dad's going
to say no. But when I tell
him what HP means to Cal,
he goes all soft and gives the okay.

When I knock on Cal's door,
he doesn't respond right
away. I figure his music is too
loud, so this time I pound.

> *Coming!* he yells. *Hold on.*

The look on his face when
he opens up is annoyed,
and I'm tempted to change
my mind. Instead, I smile.

"Wanna watch *Fantastic Beasts*?"

I'm not allowed screen time.

"I talked Mom and Dad into it.
Still no video games, but TV is okay."

His expression morphs.
He can't believe it.

Why? I thought you hated me.

"I only hate you a little.
And I thought you'd like the movie."

What's the catch?

Catch. Right. I should've
thought of a catch. "You have
to do my homework for a month."

Thanks, but no thanks. I'll pass.

"Just kidding. Come on."

Mom has cut what's left
of the Super Combo
into bite-size squares.

She sets two stacked plates
on the coffee table.

Less mess this way, she says.

Hey, I'm a big boy now, says Dad.
I can handle man-size slices.

But it's all in fun.
No arguments allowed.

Cal doesn't say much.
I think he's still suspicious.

But he pops pizza bites
along with the rest of us,
and laughs where
he should at the movie.

It's not totally relaxed.
Something feels
a little uneasy.

Kind of like sitting
in a small rowboat
while the ocean rolls
and swells beneath it.

But none of us drown.

The movie's good.
   The pizza's gone.
      The mood has improved.

For once, it's like
the four of us are
a regular family,
all watching TV,
none of us angry
or upset.

   Until I climb into bed.

FACT OR FICTION:
I Forgot About the Pine Cones

Answer: Unfortunately, true.

Look. I snuck them in Hannah's
bed when she was still in
the kitchen, talking about me
behind my back to her parents.

How was I supposed to know
she would turn around
and be all nice an hour later?

Is that, like, one of those
girl hormone things
they taught us about?

Because if it is, being a girl
is almost as strange as being me.

Whatever Hannah's reason,
I'm still surprised she wanted
me to be part of the family
movie thing last night.

So I was stuck in this
What just happened? space
when we all went to bed
and she started screaming.

If I'd remembered the pine cones
sooner, everything would be
better right now. Sometimes pranks
that seem perfectly fine when you pull
them go totally wrong in the end.

FACT OR FICTION:
This Is the First Birthday Party I've Ever Been To

Answer: Easy one, right?

I have never, ever, before
this day been invited
to a birthday party,
unless you count the ones
my mom threw for herself.

Upside:
>   never had to buy a gift.

Downside:
>   think of all the cake I missed.

I had no clue what Brylee
would like, so I chipped in
some allowance, and Hannah
picked out her presents.

Hopefully my name is still
on one of them. Hannah's mad
at me again. She makes that
clear by staring out the window.

>   Another silent car ride.
>   *All my fault again.*
>   No apology can fix it.

I should probably quit, like,
apologizing. As Hannah said,
sorry doesn't mean anything
if you keep having to repeat it.

FACT OR FICTION:
I'm a Champion Roller Skater

Answer: Ha ha ha ha ha.

When I was really little,
I got a pair of those cheap
plastic skates, and I *was*
pretty good. On carpet.

Took them outside once.
Too bad I didn't have knee
and elbow pads. Mom
couldn't afford both,
though they probably
would've been cheaper
than all the first-aid
cream and Band-Aids.

Other than those and one
pair of Heelys, which
I actually rode well,
I've never tried roller-skating.
Counting on the Heely
experience to keep me
from looking like a klutz.

We go inside, locate the party
table, say hi to Brylee and
her mom, and park the presents,
one of which does have my name on it.

Hannah has her own skates,
but I'll have to use rentals
that look ancient.

By the time I've got them
laced, almost everyone
in our class is here and
circling the concrete rink.

Hannah and Misty
are buddied up and look
like a couple of pros.

Most of the others
are at least competent.

And then there's me.

These big, heavy skates
are not Heelys.

First time around,
down I go.

          Once.
                    Twice.
                              Argh!

Stop.
  Observe.
    Ah, chin tilted up.

Shoulders square.
    Palms toward the floor.
       Knees bent, hips flexed.

And suddenly, I see exactly
what I've been doing wrong!

FACT OR FICTION:
Skating Is About Your Feet

Answer: Well, they count for something.

But it isn't about trying
to walk with wheels.

It's about shifting
your weight from side to side.

Left.
      Right.
            Left.
                  Right.

The more I watch
the really good skaters,
the more I recognize it.
So now I try it.

It still takes a couple
of times around
to get the hang of it,
but then it clicks.

Left.
      Right.
            Left.
                  Right.

It's sort of like math.
Once you understand
the basic skills, you get
the correct answers.
It even starts to be fun.

I don't try anything
fancy, like backward
skating, or the games
they do, like limbo.

But they're playing
good music, and when
I move to the rhythm,
it makes it even easier.

At one point, I skate
past Hannah and Misty,
who are standing at
the railing, and I hear
Hannah comment,

Don't you think he's cute?

Pretty sure they're not
talking about me.

I glance around, trying
to figure out who
Hannah's crushing on.

Vic? Nope.
Bradley? No way.
(I can't believe they're here!)

Sam or Justin or Troy?
Maybe.

Oh. Wait. I know who it is.
Tripp Wilson.

FACT OR FICTION:
I've Seen Hannah Smile at Tripp

Answer: Uh, yeah.

And in a weird, kind of
creepy way. I guess maybe
I realized what that smile meant.

I mean, you see it all
the time on TV and in movies.

I just never thought
about Hannah
liking someone that way.

I've got a word for such
information: *ammunition*.

But I won't fire it today.
I'll store it away.

No, today is about Brylee,
and now they're calling us
over for pizza (again!)
and birthday cake (finally!).

There are a lot of us.
Twenty-two kids and a few
adults who chose to stay,
including Aunt Taryn.

She's friends with Brylee's
mom, but mostly she hung
out to provide supervision.
I'm who's on her mind.

But no trouble from me
so far. She really ought
to keep an eye on Hannah,
who's totally checking out
Tripp Wilson, who's a lot
more interested in pepperoni.

It takes a half hour
to turn the pizza and cake
into crumbs on our plates,
and then Brylee gets to open
her presents. Man, what a haul!

Games. Books. Craft sets.
A karaoke machine from her mom.
And lots of clothes.

In fact, Hannah gives her
a cool Captain Marvel
sweatshirt.

> Vic, of course, decides to be
> mean. *Captain Marvel. Right.*
> *Like a girl could be a superhero.*

Yeah, adds Bradley. *Stupid.*

I should be quiet, but . . .
"Not only could Captain
Marvel kick both your butts,
but I bet Brylee could, too."

Some kids laugh. Others
look concerned. This could
go a couple of ways.

Luckily, Brylee's mom
interrupts.
                    Bry is my superhero.
                    And here's her last present.

Last but not least, it's
my contribution. Everyone
except Vic and Bradley
(who are glaring at me)
watches Brylee open it.

And the big reveal is . . .
                              hair chalk!

I definitely would not
have picked that out.

Doesn't matter. Brylee
is really sweet when
        she says, *Thank you, Cal.*
        I've wanted that forever.

Hannah knows a thing
or two about her friend.
Hair chalk. Go figure.
Right up there with fingernail
polish and lip gloss.

Definitely strange being a girl.

FACT OR FICTION:
Bullies Don't Pick on Girls

Answer: Bullies pick on anyone.

As long as they think
someone is weaker,
that person is at risk.

Today, not only is that person
a girl, but she happens
to be the birthday girl.

We're skating again.
Brylee's a little in front of me
when the creeps zoom past.
Bradley bumps me on purpose.
I lose my balance and hit
the floor. Hard.

I'm getting up, face hot
and right leg throbbing, when Vic
skates up behind Brylee.

> *Hey! Captain Marvel!*
> *I hear you can fly.*

He yanks on the back
of her shirt and she windmills
her arms to keep from falling.

Okay, who other than Vic
and Bradley would have fun
at a party, then harass
the person who invited them?

Definition of *Road Rage*:
Aggressive Behavior by a Driver on a Road

Apparently, there is also such
a thing as rink rage, because
we're watching it right now.

For once, I don't blame Cal.
What is wrong with Bradley
and Vic? They deserve
whatever Cal has in mind
as he goes after them.

I poke Misty. "Look how
good he's skating."

I don't think he's been on
skates before. Today,
his first time around,
he fell at least three times.

Yeah, I laughed. Out loud.
After the pine cone thing,
it was kind of like payback.

Misty nods. *It's weird how
fast he figured it out.*

"Pretty sure he learned
just by watching other people."

His brain might be scrambled.
But sometimes it works
above average.

So, in one afternoon
he's gone from limping
around the oval to full-on
rink rage maneuvers.

After checking on Brylee,

he zips around a couple
of people, then catches
up to Vic, who isn't looking
behind him and doesn't
see what's coming.

> *Dude!* Cal yells loud enough
> to be heard over the music.
> *What is wrong with you?*

You can tell Vic's surprised.
No one ever confronts him.
He pivots toward Cal. Stops.
Pulls himself up super tall,
and the look on his face
is the meanest ever.

Everyone moves away
from the two of them,
expecting a fight.
Well, everyone except
Bradley, who turns
around to join in.

Uh-oh, says Misty. *Two on one.*
Maybe we should get your mom.

"Good idea." But again,
we don't get the chance,
because by the time we reach
that side of the rink,

stuff

has

happened.

Definition of *Shiner*:
Black Eye

Pretty sure that's what Cal
has coming. A big ol' shiner.

Vic's fists are raised.
And Bradley has circled
behind Cal, where he can
easily keep him from
defending himself.

Cal understands the risk,
but this time he's ready
and in control.

I'm close enough now
to hear him say,

> *Brylee was nice enough*
> *to invite you to her party.*
> *Maybe you should apologize.*

> Vic moves into him.
> *You gonna make me?*

Here comes the shiner.
But, no. Maybe not.

Cal shakes his head
and keeps his voice low.

I'm not going to mess up
Brylee's birthday. Neither
should you guys, okay?

He skates away.
Vic's jaw drops.
Bradley looks confused.

Definition of *Civility*:
Politeness

Cal goes over to Brylee.
>He says something to her.
>>She nods and smiles.

Now they're skating.
>Next to each other.
>>Like they're friends.

"What just happened?"
I can't believe Cal pulled it off.

>*I'm not sure*, says Misty.
>*But Vic and Bradley look*
>*like they wonder, too.*

They stand there.
>Shaking their heads.
>>Considering their next move.

Bradley seems to decide.
>He gestures to Vic.
>>Unbelievably, they leave.

No apology, but that's okay.
It's better than a fight.

"What did Ms. Crowell say
about dealing with bullies?
Baffle them with civility?"

Something like that. But
who knew it would work?

I guess grown-ups know
some stuff. I file that away
for the future. But now

Misty asks the question
I've been trying not
to think too hard about.

So, what's up with Brylee
and Cal? They look . . . close.

They're not, like, touching.
But I know what she means.
And, yeah, it bugs me.

"Wonder how she'd feel
about pine cones in her bed."

What? Misty hasn't heard
the story yet.

I tell it to her now and
it makes her laugh.

You have to admit, his
torture is creative.

"But it hurt, and that was after
I talked Mom and Dad into
letting him watch a movie
with us, despite every messed-up
thing he did yesterday."

That's because you're nice.

That should make me feel
good. Instead, I feel rotten
because Brylee is *my* friend.

Why was Cal the one who
tried to make her feel better?

Definition of *Diversion*:
An Activity That Draws Your Attention

I want to think about something
else, so I divert my brain waves
by watching Tripp Wilson.

He isn't too tall, but he is kind
of buff, a rad skater (well,
blader—he's using
fancy K2 in-line skates) and
not bad to look at, either.

Misty agrees, though she says
his dark brown hair is too long
and I'm crazy to worry about
liking him, anyway.

> *Between school and dance*
> *and gymnastics, when do*
> *you even have time to*
> *think about boys?*

"I'm not really thinking
about him. I'm just admiring
his rugged good looks."

That makes us laugh
because my mom said that
once about this old-time
actor named Marlon Brando.

I've watched a couple
of his movies with her, and
I guess he was kind of cute,
at least when he was young.

But not as cute as Tripp,
who doesn't pay any
attention to me at all.
That's bad and good.

Good because if he noticed
me staring, I'd be mortified.
Bad because why isn't he at
least a little bit interested?

Is there, like, something
wrong with me?

Misty seems to know
what I'm thinking.

> *Why don't you go ask him*
> *to show you how to do*
> *a trick or something?*

I'm kind of considering
it when the music goes quiet
and an announcement
comes over the speaker.

Everyone except Brylee
Parker, please clear the floor.
And, Brylee, please come
to the center of the rink.

By the time the floor
empties, the party hostess
has joined Brylee mid-oval.
She brought a bouquet
of multicolored balloons.

We're going to play a game,
she says into her microphone.
I have twelve balloons here, and
to win a prize, you have to pop
them all in sixty seconds or less.

Sounds easy enough.

It's harder than it might seem.
So, find a couple of friends.
If you go twenty seconds without
popping three, tag your pals in.

I totally expect her to pick
Misty and me. Uh, no.
Cal and—get this—Tripp
meet her center rink and wait.

The hostess hands a balloon
to Brylee, sets her stopwatch.
On your mark. Get set . . . Go!

First Brylee tries squeezing,
but the balloon must not be
very full, because air just
squishes up into one end.

Sit on it! yells Cal.

She does, and it works,
but ten seconds have gone by
and she's only popped one.

Tag!

Cal and Tripp are a lot
more aggressive.

Pop! Pop!
    Pop! Pop!
        Pop! Pop!
            Pop! Pop!
                Pop! Pop!

Brylee makes it twelve just in time.

Definition of *Petty*:
Small-minded; Mean-spirited

Brylee has to share
her prize—three coupons
for free skate sessions,
including rentals
and refreshments.

No big gain.
        No big loss.
                No big deal.

Still, when Brylee skates
over to Misty and me,
I'm kind of cross and
maybe a little whiny
when I ask, "Why did
you pick Cal and Tripp?"

> *Because they're boys
> and I figured they'd be
> good at popping balloons.
> Boys are always breaking
> things, aren't they?*

Her answer makes sense.
Cal, for one, has broken
a lot of things, sometimes
accidentally, other
times totally on purpose.

"Okay, I get it."

But she understands
I feel hurt.

> *Do you want my free*
> *skate session coupon?*

Now I feel petty.

I know that's not how
she wants me to feel.
Her offer was simple kindness.
Because that's the kind
of person she is.

I tell her, "No. That's okay.
You guys earned it.
But thanks anyway."

> *Please don't be mad.*

"I'm not. I promise. Come
on. Let's skate."

We circle the rink again.
This time, it's Misty, Brylee
and me, and that feels good,
like how things should be.

I don't even mind
when Cal skates up behind
us, joins the group.

Especially
because
he brought
Tripp with him.

FACT OR FICTION:
Hannah's Jealous of Me

Answer: Pretty sure that's a big affirmative.

It's been four days
since Brylee's party,
and anytime I talk
to her at school, Hannah
shoots me a wicked glare.

She never said so, but I think
it bugged her when Brylee
picked Tripp and me to play
the balloon game.

He and I killed it! I'm glad
we did, because no one
ever picks me. Like, ever.

And after finally being
chosen, it would have been
embarrassing to let Brylee down.

It meant a lot that she wanted
me, even if it was only because
she guessed I'd be a good popper.

Hannah told me that, and
she said it kind of snotty.

That's the reason I think
she's jealous. What I can't
figure out is why.

Everything is "hers."

> *Her*
> > > home.
> *Her*
> > > school.
> *Her*
> > > parents.

It's not like I'm trying
to steal them.

Living here wasn't even
my choice. Not that I'm
ungrateful. I like it here,
and I hope I can stay.

In fact, the idea of leaving
makes my stomach hurt,
kind of like it remembers
being empty too often.

But I'm definitely not greedy.

When you come from
a place where there
isn't much good,
finding a decent home
is a total surprise.

But Hannah doesn't have
to worry about losing
anything to me.

That includes her friends.

FACT OR FICTION:
Math Is My Best Subject

Answer: By far.

I'm okay at English,
mostly because I read
so much, but I don't really
like to write unless
I can make weird stuff up.

Essays? Reports?
Not so much.

And anything autobiographical
rates a big nope from me.

Social studies is boring.
Science is cool, I guess.

But math has always
been super easy
because the rules don't change.
Learn 'em once,
you're good to go.

Right now, we're graphing
two variable equations
on the coordinate plane,
which is easier than it sounds.

Our math teacher,
Mr. Shorter, is helping
Misty when Tripp complains,
            I don't get it.

I've already finished
my worksheet, so I go over

to see if I can help.
"What's the problem?"

            Tripp shrugs. *I don't*
            know where to start.

"Let me show you."
It takes a couple
of minutes, but finally
he knows what to do.

            Wow. Thanks, man.
            Wanna be my tutor?

                  As if, says Hannah,
                  passing by on her way
                  to the pencil sharpener.

            Tripp looks at me.
            What's her problem?

"Who knows?"

He grins. *She's cute*
but kind of stuck-up.

File that away, too.
Info like that just might
come in handy.

Mr. Shorter *ahems.*
Please pass your worksheets
forward. If any of you are still
having trouble, see me at break.

A couple of kids moan
and he adds,
It's my break, too, you know.
I'd rather sip a latte, myself.

Tripp gives me a thumbs-up,
meaning thanks for rescuing
his recess. Afterward,
we're back with Mrs. Peabody,
who's all excited about a project.

Thanksgiving is next week,
and this year, we're going
to try something new.

One thing most people feel
thankful for is their family.
I want you to research
your genealogical history.

Were your ancestors indigenous?
If not, where did they come
from, and when did they arrive
in America? Where did they settle?

Those questions lead to two
assignments—a one-page story
with the answers for social (boring)
studies, and for ELA, a three-
generation (big nope) family tree.

FACT OR FICTION:
I Can't Stand Family Gatherings

Answer: Depends.

They can be amusing,
but it kind of matters who all's
there and what mood you're in.

We used to have summer
family reunions. Mom's family
only, never my dad's.
Mostly, they were fun.

The kids, like Hannah
and me, played while
the grown-ups drank
and talked and once
in a while got into fights.

Sometimes I got bored,
and then I'd think up decent
pranks. Like one time—it was
the summer before Mom got
sick, so I must've been seven—
I spiked the punch.

      With hot sauce.
            A whole bottle.

I'm not sure how, but someone
figured out it was me who did it.

I got into major trouble.
                    That wasn't so much fun.

Some adults can't seem
to find a sense of humor.

Especially when spicy stuff
goes right through them
and the nearest bathroom
is clear across the park.

So, yeah, things got serious
real fast, especially
for Grandma Campbell.
I guess she made it
to the bathroom okay.

But she was gone a long time,
and when she came back,
her cheeks were red and creased
and she got right up in my face.

                    You did this, didn't you?

Her breath smelled like onions,
hot sauce and beer. I gagged,
but she kept on going.

The apple doesn't fall far
from the tree, and you'll end
up in prison, just like your father.

Mom wrapped her arms
around me, and I hid my eyes
in the soft folds of her shirt.

Stop it, Mama. Leave Cal
alone. He's just a child.

FACT OR FICTION:
Mom and Grandma Didn't Get Along

Answer: True, and it was because of Dad.

I guess I already knew that,
but that day, Grandma made it clear.

She talked *about* Mom, not *to* her,
so everyone could hear.

> *You should've stayed in college.*
> *You could've been somebody.*

> *But now look at you. Jailbird*
> *husband, barely making ends meet.*

> *Working a dead-end job and raising*
> *a kid on your own. No wonder . . .*

Every word hurt Mom, I could
tell. But still, she looked Grandma

straight in the eye.
> *No wonder what, Mama?*

> *No wonder that boy is a brat.*
> *The child needs better supervision.*

"No, I don't!" I yelled, even
if it might have been true.

He's rude, she said, like I wasn't
even there. *Terrible parenting.*

I wriggled out of Mom's hug,
put my hands on my hips.

"You be quiet. She's the best
mom in the whole universe!"

That made a few people laugh,
including Mom. But not Grandma.

They didn't say anything else
to each other. Not that day.

If they spoke at all after
that, I never knew about it.

The next time I saw Grandma
was at Mom's funeral.

But later, in the motel after
the reunion, I started thinking.

"Hey, Mom. Do you like your job?"
She worked at a grocery store.

> *It's okay. The people are nice.*
> *I wish it paid better, though.*

I thought some more. "Why
didn't you stay in college?"

She sighed. *I met your dad and fell
in love. He wanted me to drop out.*

"That wasn't fair. Why did you
listen? You should've said no!"

*But then I wouldn't have you.
And I love you more than any career.*

That made me feel a little better.
Another question popped into my head.

"So, when you were young,
what did you want to be?"

FACT OR FICTION:
Mom Wanted to Be a Nurse

Answer: No. She wanted to be an actress.

Up until that moment,
I had no idea that she watched
old movies to "learn from the greats,"
or that she got all the leads
in her high school plays.

I felt happy that she told me,
but also a little sad.
What other secrets was Mom
hiding? What else didn't I know?

I knew my dad was in prison
for drugs and stolen property,
not to mention knocking Mom
and me around.

My earliest memories are sounds
    slammed doors
        punched walls
            screaming.

Mom and Dad fought. A lot.
Sometimes things got physical
    shoving
        scratching
            hitting.

I saw
       bloodied lips and noses
                purple welts and bruises.

After one epic battle, Dad passed
out. Mom hustled me to her car.

Just as she started it, he came
running and tried to stop us.

The doors were locked, but he
jerked the handles anyway.
His foot was behind the front
tire and Mom ran right over it.

I'll never forget his rage-puffed
face or the curses he screamed.
And then he lifted his right hand.

In it was a gun.
Pretty sure it was loaded.

If he'd pulled the trigger,
he would've killed Mom,
and maybe me.

She thought so, too, and that's
what she said as we drove away.

After three days in a shelter,
she crawled right on back.

He's only like this once in a while
was part of her lame excuse.
It's better not to disrupt our lives—
your school, my work . . . was the rest.

Which meant I had to go back, too.
I wasn't sure how to feel.
I hated my dad for hurting us.
I loved him because he was my dad.

FACT OR FICTION:
Both Were True

Answer: Both were true then.

This is true today:

Now I hate my dad
for hurting me.

I don't think
I could ever
love him again.

In fact,
I don't ever
want to see
him again.

So, after school,
what Aunt Taryn
says makes me
want to disappear.

Definition of *Ashen*:
Pale; Gray

When Cal and I get home
from school, Mom has news.
The look on her face
says it can't be good.

"What's wrong?" I ask.

She puts a hand
on Cal's shoulder.

> *I heard from your father today.*
> *He's out of prison.*

Cal's face fades to ashen
and he loses his smile.

> *Oh* is all he says.

> *He's asking for visitation.*

> *No!*

Mom tries to give him
a hug, but Cal jerks away.

> *I don't want to see him!*

> *I don't think we have a choice,*
> *although we can request*
> *any visits to be supervised.*

When can we go to court?
Can't I please tell the judge no?

Cal bolts from the room
without waiting for an answer.

Mom takes a deep breath.

> *Poor kid. Glad I didn't tell*
> *him my other news.*

"There's more?"

She nods.

> *Guess who decided to*
> *grace our Thanksgiving*
> *table with her presence.*

Thanksgiving is next week.
I can only think of a couple
of "her"s who might join us.

"Grandma?"

> *Good guess. She said it's been*
> *too long since she's seen*
> *you and Cal, and she'll bring*
> *her famous pecan pie.*

I'm not really big on pecans,
and Grandma Campbell
isn't always the easiest
person to get along with,
though she and I do okay.

But for Cal?
Wow. That's, like,
double bad news.
Contentious, even.

Definition of *Contentious*:
Hostile; Unfriendly

If I didn't know what
contentious meant, thinking
back to Aunt Caryn's funeral,
I could figure it out.

The family all sat up front.

Grandpa Campbell
was on one side of the aisle.

Grandma was on the other.

They barely even looked
at each other.
Divorce does that.

Next to Grandma was Mom,
and beside her was Cal.
Grandma didn't talk to him, either.

Cal's dad, David, sat in back.
No one wanted him there,
and he knew it.

You couldn't not notice
how every once in a while
Grandma turned to glare.

Cal sat, stiff and quiet,
through the whole thing.
He didn't even cry until
they closed the casket.

Then, when they covered
her face and started to wheel
that shiny copper box away,
he totally freaked out.

It was like, right until then,
she was still there,
even if she was dead.

      No! Cal yelled. *Leave her alone!*

He ran to the front of the chapel,
started tugging on the minister's sleeve.
Then he dropped to his knees.

      Please don't take her away.

That's when his dad
came forward.

I'd only seen him
a couple of times before
and he looked different.

Still tall and handsome,
I thought, but . . .
                    Scraggly.
                              Worn-out.
                                        Empty.

He took charge of Cal.

                    Come on. Get up off the floor.
                    You can't change what is.

Cal resisted, so his dad
lifted him up and held
him long enough
to let the pallbearers roll
the casket down the aisle.

Then Uncle David carried Cal,
kicking and spitting,
out the door.

I felt so sorry for Cal,
it actually hurt,
like all the air got sucked
from my lungs.

Everyone was watching.
Some people sniffled.

A few were whispering,
and I could only guess
they were talking about
that poor boy who
just lost his mother.

Mom was sobbing.
Dad held her close,
trying to soothe her.

But Grandma?
Her face was blank,
though maybe her eyes
sparkled with a few tears
as she turned to make sure
Cal and his dad were gone.

Then she said something,
and the freezing-cold tone
of her voice made me shiver.

*Good riddance. I never
want to see that man again.*

And, I wondered,
what about Cal?

Definition of *Empathy*:
Understanding; Sympathy

Wow. Look at me, finding
empathy for Cal.
That isn't always easy,
but I'm getting better at it.

I know he won't be happy
about our Thanksgiving visitor.

Grandma is kind of hard
to understand.

When Aunt Caryn was sick
and Mom went to Phoenix
to help out, Grandma stayed
here to take care of me
when Dad had to work.

Mostly, she was nice,
but a little cool,
like she didn't want
to get too close.

And once in a while,
she drank too much wine.
Then she'd either say mean
things about people
or go completely silent,
like she was thinking
about things that hurt.

"Hey, Mom. Maybe
Grandma and Cal will
decide they like each other."

I'd love that, Hannah.

"What about Cal's dad?
Will he try to get Cal back?"

I don't know. It's possible.
But I'd hope he wants
what's best for his son.

"Is living with us best?"

Considering Cal's reaction,
I'd have to say yes.

Uh, yeah. Good point.

Mom glances at her watch.

Dance practice in forty-five
minutes. Any homework?

"A little math and reading,
but I can do that in the car.
Oh, and I have to work on
researching a family tree."

I can help you with that.
It might take a little time,
though. When is it due?

"Next Tuesday, along with
a paper about our ancestors.
Where they came from and stuff."

It's Thursday, so we've got five
days. Dad's home this weekend,
so he can help you with his side.

Oh. Wait. Cal has to do this, too?
Because that's going to be tough.

Definition of *Privileged*:
Favored; Lucky

Oh, man. I didn't think
about that, and I bet
Mrs. Peabody didn't, either,
when she made up this assignment.

I can know everything
about both sides of my family
because I can talk to both
of my parents about where
their ancestors came from.

But Cal's dad isn't around,
so how's he supposed to
find out that information?

I guess that makes me
more privileged, which
is weird. It's hard to look
at myself that way.

I used to think when people
said someone was privileged,
it meant they were rich.
Like, they owned

> giant diamonds
> fur coats
> mansions
> or maybe even
> a jet or a yacht.

Now I know better.

Mom told me privilege
isn't just what you have.
It's about who you are.

> *Privilege is living in safer*
> *neighborhoods and going*
> *to better schools. It's being*
> *able to give your kids music*
> *lessons or dance classes—*

"Wait," I'd interrupted. "I get
to take dance and gymnastics.
But we're not privileged, are we?"

> *Your dad has an excellent job,*
> *and that gives us a level*
> *of privilege many others*
> *will never enjoy.*

"Dad has to work really
hard, though."

> *Yes. But some people have*
> *to work two or even three jobs*
> *just to cover rent and food*
> *because they're not paid very well.*

It must be hard to be
an adult and know stuff
like that. Probably why
they worry so much.

I'd rather just stay a kid
for a while.

Definition of *Contemplate*:
Think About

Still, I think it's better
to have answers you need
than have to wonder
about them.

I contemplated what Mom
said, and now I understand
more about some other
kids I know from school.

That includes Cal.

I bet we'd be more
alike if our moms hadn't
made totally different choices.

Like, my mom and dad
got together and decided
to live in this house,
in a nice neighborhood,
in this quiet little suburb.

But Aunt Caryn married
Uncle David, and they moved
into an apartment in a rough
area of a huge, noisy city.

       I got dance classes.
              Cal got the school playground.

I got gymnastics.
                    Cal got video games.

I got Disneyland.
                    Cal got the Boys & Girls Club.

I guess that wasn't so bad.
Cal told me that's where
he learned to shoot pool,

play chess and basketball.

But he's never been
                    to Disneyland.

And for now, he only
                    has half of a family.

The half we share.
What I'm starting to see
is that he and I like a lot
of the same things because
our moms did, too.

          I like Italian food.
                    Cal likes it, too.

          I love old movies.
                    Cal loves them, too.

I adore great books.
Cal adores them, too.

And maybe if we'd grown up
the same way, we'd appreciate
each other more, too.

Okay, maybe,
maybe not.

Definition of *Force Field*:
Invisible Shield of Energy

In the back seat on the way
to dance, Cal stares out
the window and won't talk.

I ask him questions
about our math homework,
but he has surrounded
himself with a force field
that I can't break through.

When we get to the studio
and Mom parks the car,
I try to pierce it one more time.

"Hey, Cal? Don't worry.
Everything will be okay."

   Sure.

He says it without looking
at me, and I'm halfway
irritated when he turns.

   Thanks, Hannah.

     She's right, Cal, says Mom.
     We'll make it be okay.

   Uh-huh.

I don't think he's convinced.

In class, I try to concentrate
on my routine. Next month
is our holiday recital
and I want every step
to be just right.

But I keep glancing
over at Cal, who, of course,
is reading. I hope the book
can take him somewhere
else for a while.

I love my dad so much.
I can't imagine
not wanting
to see him.

Or being
afraid of him.

Dance is all about counting.
One-two-three-four,
each movement numbered.
I miscount a few times,
stumble through the routine.

> *Everything okay, Hannah?*
> asks Mrs. Bell, my teacher.

"Yeah. Sorry. Just some
stuff on my mind."

But not nearly as much
as what's on Cal's mind.

He stays wrapped
in his force field
all the way home,
and through dinner.

He doesn't even flinch
when he finds out about
our Thanksgiving visitor.

Definition of *Genetics*:
The Study of Genes and Heredity

Our heredity project also
has a science element.
Friday morning, we learn
that every living creature
has these things inside
them called genes.

They're made from this stuff
called DNA, which is like
a code that decides
how a person looks and
whether they might be
at risk for some diseases.

Half your DNA comes from
your mother, the other
half from your father,
explains our science teacher.

Siblings who share a mom
but have different dads
might not look too much alike.

Vic decides to stir things up.
What about Hannah and Cal?
They had different moms
but they look alike. Does that
mean they had the same dad?

Cal and I yell in unison.

"No!"   *No!*

I look at Misty. "Do Cal
and I actually look alike?"

She nods a giant *yes.*

Not everyone knows,
so I tell them, "Cal's mom
and my mom were identical twins."

That leads to a discussion
about twins and DNA.

I only half listen and spend
the time glancing at Cal,
who keeps staring back at me.

His hair is curly.
          Mine's kind of wavy.
                    But they're the same color.

He's got lots of freckles.
          I've only got a few.
                    But we both have them.

His eyes are the color of honey.
         Mine are a shade darker.
                 But basically, they're brown.

All those things
        came
            from our mothers.

So I guess what's different—
Cal's taller, narrower,
and has a little bump
on his nose—must've come
from our fathers.

Who knew biology
could be so interesting?

FACT OR FICTION:
Some Italian People Have Red Hair

Answer: Apparently so.

I figured the "ginger"
family coloring came from
Grandpa Campbell's Scottish
roots, and they might be
responsible for some of it.

But what Hannah and I
learn from Aunt Taryn is,
her mother's Rossi relatives
are from northern Italy,
and many also have red hair.

That includes the Wicked
Witch of the North herself.
Funny, I thought it was
just because she dyed it.

Anyway, it's Sunday, and
we're working on the maternal
side of our projects.

> So, our Campbell kin landed
> in America in the early 1800s.
> Some stayed in Massachusetts,
> but others migrated west.
>
> The Rossi side arrived not long
> before the Civil War and settled
> in the New York area . . .

There's a lot more information.
Aunt Taryn knows most of the details
about her family, and I guess
it's good for me to know them, too.

I don't want my paper to be
too much like Hannah's, though,
so I'll get a little creative.

Uncle Bruce already helped
Hannah with his side.
That stuff is useless to me,
though she's happy to learn
about the Lincolns.

They came to this country
from Lincolnshire, England,
and washed up on American soil
(literally—their ship-to-shore
rowboat capsized in the harbor)
in 1685. Good thing they could swim.

As for my paternal ancestry,
I told Mrs. Peabody
I didn't know much about it.

She said to do the best
I could, which kind of gives me
permission to make everything
up, and that's my plan.

FACT OR FICTION:
The Name Pace Means "Fast"

Answer: Sounds right, but no.

Aunt Taryn looked it up.
It comes from a Latin word
that means "peace."

It doesn't fit.

Not me.
Not Dad.
Not Uncle Frank.

According to Aunt Taryn's research,
the name Pace seems to be British,
and my ancestors probably
immigrated from England,
but I have no clue when.

All I know about my dad's
family is, his parents
are—or were—farmers.
I'm not sure where.

When Dad turned eighteen,
he had a big fight with
his father and hitchhiked
to California. At least,
that's what he told me.

If I never smell tractor
oil and manure again,
it will be too soon, he said.

I asked about my grandparents
exactly once after that.

Dad's evil glare
made me understand
I should never bring up
the subject again.

I admit when he went to prison
the first time, I asked Mom
if she'd ever met them.
I couldn't help wondering
about who they were.

Never, she said. *Something*
very bad happened between
your dad and his parents.
He won't tell me what it was,
but I think it was worse
than a shouting match.

She didn't even know their names,
and at that point, she didn't care.

I can't say for sure, but
as far as I know, they haven't
come looking for your father.
There must be a reason for that.

"What if they're dead?"
I'm not sure why that
crossed my mind, but it did.

Hopefully then they're at peace.
I don't think they care
to connect with him. Or us.

Maybe I'll track them down
someday.

It might be cool
to meet them.

But maybe they're weirdos.

Family
is such
a complicated
thing.

I doubt
I want
a bigger one,
especially
on the Pace side.

For my project, I'll create
a colorful collection of kin.
That's Aunt Taryn's
word, and I like its sound.

Let me think.

Kin
          Can
                    Con

That's good.
But a little too close to true.

FACT OR FICTION:
Hannah's Been Pretty Nice Lately

Answer: Yeah, even when I bug her.

And what's weird is, I like
it better when bugging her
gets a negative reaction.

Because that's something
I understand. I think she feels
sorry for me, and that's not okay.

Guess we'll see if my story
changes that. I worked hard
on it, all last night.

It's been kind of interesting
hearing about where
people's families came from.
Europe. Africa. Asia. South America.
None from Antarctica,
and that's too bad.
We might've gotten a penguin tale.

Hannah's is kind of plain,
but I have to admit
she did a really good job
on her family tree.
She made it an oak, with
acorns for the pictures
and names. It's neat.

Unlike mine.

My story's pretty good,
though, even without penguins:

> "I don't want to bore you
> with information you'll get
> from my cousin, who'll tell
> you about how our moms'
> relatives came from Scotland
> in 1818 and Italy in 1859.
>
> "But I'm pretty sure she won't
> go into some of the cool extra
> info, like how our great-great-
> great-great-grandpa wanted
> to go west, so he joined a cattle
> drive and had to fight bandits
> and lasso bulls and stuff—"

> > *Cal* . . . warns Hannah.

"What?"

> > *Never mind.*

> > > Totally smiling, Mrs. Peabody
> > > says, *Please continue, Cal.*

"I only know a little about
my dad's side and I couldn't
ask anyone about it, but what
I can tell you is the first Pace
came from England in the 1700s.

"He was in the navy but
didn't like the food, so he
chose a pirate's life instead.
He sailed from Florida to Jamaica,
raiding and treasure hunting.

"But then he fell in love
with a minister's daughter
and settled down in Louisiana.
He decided passing an offering
plate was safer than robbing,
so he became a preacher, too.

"There was a lot of begetting—
that's a Bible word for having
babies—and the family grew
at a really fast Pace . . ."

Not everyone gets the joke,
but there's a moan or two
that means somebody did.

And on paper, the *P*
is capitalized, so I'm sure
Mrs. Peabody will.

Hopefully she'll give me
extra credit for humor.
Considering my family tree
chart, I'll probably need it.

FACT OR FICTION:
Mrs. Peabody Encouraged Creativity

Answer: Yes, and she'll probably regret it.

Everyone did different kinds
of trees besides Hannah's oak.
Brylee, maple. Misty, apple.

Mine is a palm tree,
with coconuts for
the pictures and names.

Only, on one side
the palm fronds hang
down, limp and dead.

Under one is a drawing—
two coconuts. Dad.
And his brother.

Dad is a scribbled face.

Uncle Frank is two dots
for eyes. And teeth.

Which is the most
I've ever said about him
and I hope it
wasn't a mistake.

The other side of the tree
is mostly alive. At least,
it's green, and the fronds
arc the way they should.

There's only one deceased
coconut.

        M

         o

          m

But dead is not how
she looks. No way.

I pasted a pic
of her face there.
One from before she was sick.
One with ginger hair.

The coconut beside her
is Aunt Taryn, and it's hard
to tell them apart.
Except, not for me.

Above, to the left, hangs
coconut Grandpa Campbell.

To the right, perched
on top of the tree,
is the Wicked Grandma
of the North.

Throwing coconuts.
At Mom.
And me.

Definition of *Gobsmacked*:
Majorly Surprised

Wow.
Wow.
Wow.

That's all I've got to say
about Cal's family tree.

Pretty sure all the other kids
agree, because the room
is totally silent.

And Mrs. Peabody
looks gobsmacked,
which is a rad word.

> *Well, that's very interesting,*
> *Cal,* she says, managing
> to stay calm. *Would you*
> *like to tell us about it?*

> *Not really,* he answers.
> *But sure. Why not? Those*
> *two are my dad and his brother.*

> *Are they, like, dead?*
> asks Bradley.

> Cal shrugs. *They could be.*
> *Anyway, they are to me.*

Cal's dad isn't, for sure.
I've never heard
about his uncle, though.

> *I'm sorry to hear that,*
> says Mrs. Peabody.
> *What about the other side?*

> *Top left is Grandpa Campbell,*
> *who's Scottish, but I don't think*
> *he wears kilts or plays bagpipes.*
> *He used to be married*
> *to the witch, but not anymore.*

Cal pauses. Probably
waiting for someone to ask
why Grandma's a witch.
But no one does.

> He points to the low-hanging
> coconuts. *That's Aunt Taryn.*
> *And that's my mom.* He kind
> of chokes up. *She was an actress.*

> *Nuh-uh*, says Vic. *You made that up.*

"No, he didn't!"   *No, I didn't!*

There we go, saying the same
thing at the same time again.
Everyone cracks up.

Except Cal, who's all puffed
up, ready to fight. He starts
toward Vic. Mrs. Peabody
tries to head him off.

Brylee saves the day.
*Well, I think your mom
looked like a movie star.
Elegant.*

Definition of *Epiphany*:
A Moment of Sudden Understanding

Cal's temper deflates
like a punctured bike tire.
Pffffft. Down it goes.

I'm surprised. Cal could
have had a giant meltdown.
It's been a couple of weeks
since the last one. That's a record.

> Instead, Cal says, *Thanks, Brylee.*
> *Mom totally* was *elegant.*
> *And she* was *an actress.*

That was directed at Vic, who
turns his back, looks away.

Mrs. Peabody asks for permission
to hang the family tree charts
until after Thanksgiving.

> *I thought we'd invite a few*
> *other classes to take a peek*
> *tomorrow, if that's okay.*
> *And, don't forget, it's a half day.*

Early release
for the holiday weekend.

We take turns taping
our projects on the wall.
Mine goes next to Cal's,
and that seems right.

They sure are different,
even though some of the faces
are the same. I wonder if anyone
from the other classes will notice.

I have to admit, even
though it's kind of creepy,
Cal's is imaginative.

      Witch grandma.
           Monster uncle.

How does he come up
with stuff like that?
Yes, he goes overboard.
Like, we're related to pirates?

But the pictures of Mom
and Aunt Caryn he chose
are perfect. Side by side,
they are elegant.

Twins.

Whoa.

Just had an epiphany.

Mom and her sister were **identical**.

Aunt Caryn looked like a **movie star**.

Which means Mom **must've, too**.

At least, when **she was young**.

Why did I never see that before?

Definition of *Vicariously*:
Experienced Through Another Person

I think about Mom
        on the school bus home.

I think about Mom
        instead of concentrating
        on my homework.

I think about Mom
        as I watch her cook pasta
        fagioli—this yummy Italian
        soup. It smells so good,
        my stomach growls *thank you.*

"Is that Grandma's recipe?"
Why did I ask?
I already know the answer.

      Yes, it is. One thing about
      my mother, she's always
      loved to cook, especially
      classic Old World recipes.

I stare at Mom
        as she ladles the soup
        into big bowls.

I stare at Mom
        as she slices sourdough
        bread and stacks
        it on a plate.

I stare at Mom
        as she sets the table.
        Three places. Dad's in Utah
        until tomorrow.
        Grandma will be here then, too.

Finally, Mom notices
how I keep looking at her.

      Is something wrong?
      Do I have a booger
      hanging out of my nose?

"Nah. I'd tell you about
that. Wouldn't want it
to drop in my soup."

      She laughs. *Two rules*
      in my kitchen. Clean hands.
      And booger-free nostrils.
      So, if I don't need a tissue,
      why are you staring at me?

"I was just thinking
how pretty you are.
Did you ever want
to be an actress?"

Maybe for about fifteen
minutes. But I actually wanted
to dance professionally.

"Why didn't you?"

Same reason Caryn moved
to Arizona. I fell in love and got
married. I worked at a bank
when Dad was still in college.
It helped pay the bills.

Ugh. I mean, I'm glad she met
Dad, but this bothers me.
Girls should do what they want,
even if they fall in love.

"But after Dad graduated,
you could've danced, right?"

It was too expensive, with no
promise that I could make
it professionally. Besides,
I needed to take care of you.

Great. It's my fault.
"But you could've gone
back after I got bigger."

*Maybe. But even when you
were really little, your own
ability was clear, so we chose
to invest there instead.*

*Listen, you impress me
more and more every day.
Not only your talent.
Your dedication and drive.*

*I'm still dancing, by the way.
Vicariously, which means
through watching you.*

"That doesn't sound like
as much fun as doing
it yourself."

*You'd be surprised.
Now, would you please
call Cal to dinner?
The soup's getting cold.*

Definition of *Cooperate*:
Work Together; Do What Someone Asks

Cal comes to the table
wearing a shallow smile.
But he loses it quickly.

He slurps a big spoonful
of delicious soup and is
swallowing when Mom says,

> *I contacted our attorney today,*
> *Cal. He's going to set a court date.*
> *Meanwhile, he says you should talk*
> *to your dad, see if he'll cooperate.*

Cal's whole body
turns to concrete.

> *What if he won't?* he asks.

> *Then things get a little more*
> *complicated. But the lawyer thinks*
> *we have a strong case, regardless.*

> *Do I have to see Dad, or can*
> *I just talk to him on the phone?*

> *We'll start with a call, but*
> *not until after the weekend.*

I hope Cal's dad will cooperate.
Cal doesn't look convinced,
but he still has an appetite.
He even asks for seconds.

Honestly, I'm surprised.
I expected a giant meltdown.
I'm thinking about that
when Mom says,

> *Hannah, when you get up*
> *tomorrow, please strip*
> *your bed so I can put on*
> *clean sheets for Grandma.*

Before I can say okay,
Cal surprises me.

> *She can have my room.*

He surprised Mom, too.

> *Oh, Cal. Are you sure?*

> *It's okay. I don't mind.*

A grin creeps across his face.
I can see his brain working.

He's probably trying to figure
out what to put in the bed
to make her scream.

Something pokey
            like pine cones?
Something slimy
            like worms?
Something jumpy
            like frogs?

At least it's giving him
something to think about
besides his father.

Definition of *Erode*:
Crumble; Decay

Cal seemed happy enough
the rest of last night,
through dessert and TV.

But when we get to school
this morning and the visiting
classes come in to look
at our family trees, it's easy
to see his mood

       E

           R

               O

                   D

                       E

and by lunch, it has slipped
from dusky to dark,
like night over a sunset.

I don't know if it's because
he's thinking about his dad
or about Grandma's visit,
but he pulls inside his shell.

As we wait for the early-
release bell, most of the kids
are laughing and talking.

Not Cal.

His face is buried
in a book, his usual
place to hide out.

Wonder how many
he'll read this weekend.

Definition of *Upbeat*:
Cheerful; Positive

Dad gets home late afternoon.
It was a short trip this time—
only two days—and he should
be upbeat, especially because
tomorrow's Turkey and Pie Day.

Instead, he seems tense.
When Mom asks how
everything went, he snaps,

> *Fine. Scratch that. Great.*
> *Does that surprise you?*

I don't get why he's so mad,
and from her expression,
I guess Mom doesn't, either.

> *Of course not*, she says.
> *I was just—*

> *Making small talk. I know.*
> *It's what you do best.*

Before Mom can respond,
the doorbell rings. Three times.

It's Grandma, holding her pecan pie
and complaining about her five-hour
(*should've been four, but traffic!*)
drive from Santa Barbara.

I haven't seen her in over
a year and she looks . . .
exactly the same as always.

She reminds me of a little tree:
spindly but tough, with hair
the color of autumn leaves.

> *Hello, hello! Can somebody*
> *please help with my luggage?*

> > *Where'd you park?* asks Dad.

> *In the driveway, of course.*

> > *You mean, behind my car?*

> *You're not going anywhere,*
> *are you?* huffs Grandma.

> > *Not immediately. I'll get your bags.*
> > *Good to see you again, Martina.*

He gives Grandma a little
kiss on the cheek, goes outside
and returns with her suitcases,
carries them to Cal's room.

> One big one.
> > One little one.
> > > One overnight bag.

Mom laughs and hugs Grandma.
Did you bring your entire wardrobe?

Careful of the pie! Took me hours.
And you know I always bring
more clothes than I need.
You can't predict the weather.

Cal, who is standing clear
across the room, whistles softly,
drawing everyone's attention.

FACT OR FICTION:
You Can't Predict the Weather

Answer: Seriously?

"Actually, you can," I tell Grandma.
"Ever heard of the Weather Service?"

I'm standing as far away
from her as I can get
and still be inside the same
room. The light through
the window makes her squint,
and every wrinkle shows.

The last time I saw her
was at Mom's funeral.

That day, she was all made up.
I even thought how weird
it was for someone that old
to wear stuff on her eyes.

But she also must have had
something that covered up
the lines on her face. Either
that or a whole lot of them
have dug into her skin
in the last three years.

Aunt Taryn shifts her weight
from one foot to the other,
a nervous dance.

But all Grandma says is,
    The Weather Service is not
    always accurate, you know.

Now she studies me like
I'm an animal at the zoo.

        It's been a long time since
        I last saw you. You've grown.

"Weird, huh? Guess you forgot
it's what happens to kids my age."

It's a test, and she knows
it. She tests me back.

        Yes, I suppose you're right.
        Slight pause. I'm surprised
        how much you look like your father.

Don't fail her test.
Don't fail her test.
But blood rushes to my face.

Can anyone but me hear
the loud *whoosh* behind
my ears? "Don't say that."

        Her eyes narrow into slits.
        Oh, I'm sorry, Cal. Are you going
        to come give me a hug?

FACT OR FICTION:
I'd Rather Hug a Snake

Answer: Even a venomous one.

I pretend to think it over.
"Maybe later," I say. As if.

Cheeks burning, I turn on one
heel and hurry out the back door.

I don't go far, just enough
to keep from freaking out.

If I did that, I'd totally fail
her test. I can't let her win.

I crash into a chair
on the patio, a place I know.

> Breathe in. Exhale slowly.
> Like my therapist taught me.

I knew it would be hard
to see her again . . .

> *I'm surprised how much*
> *you look like your father.*

She said that to be mean.
I don't believe she's sorry.

I guess I didn't really expect
things to be different between us.

But maybe I hoped they would.
Fitting in here hasn't been easy.

It took weeks to believe
I'd eat three meals every day.

Months to close my eyes
knowing I was safe in my bed.

I'd hear noises outside the window
and hide deep beneath the covers.

But, little by little, that changed.
And so have I. I'm better.

Maybe not all the way to okay.
But closer. More in control.

I still can't take feeling cornered.
I lash out. It's called self-defense.

And when too much noise
makes the walls close in, I run.

But those things don't happen
as often as they used to.

When pressure builds inside,
usually I can reverse it. That's new.

FACT OR FICTION:
If I've Changed, Others Can, Too

Answer: Probably.

But only if they want to.
It takes a lot of work.

What about Grandwitch?

I guess it's possible,
but I haven't seen it yet.

And what about Dad?

The question strikes
suddenly. Out of nowhere.

What if prison changed him?

It didn't the first time he went.
He only came out meaner.

But if he's different, what then?

I think real hard. The memories
hurt worse than a scorpion sting.

No poultice could ever soothe them.

There's nothing he can say to make
me agree to go back to him.

The wind blows up suddenly.

It bites right through my shirt,
chases me inside the house.

I go quietly.

Eavesdropping is a hobby.
I've learned a lot playing spy.

Good things and bad.

But there's nothing to hear.
Aunt Taryn's alone in the kitchen.

Uncle Bruce is unpacking.

Grandma had a long drive
and is resting before dinner.

Hannah's watching TV.

Guess I'll join her. I don't want
to think about Dad.

I don't want to think at all.

FACT OR FICTION:
Grandma Really Has Changed

Answer: Ha-ha-ha-ha-ha-ha-ha-ha-ha-ha-ha.

Except I don't feel like laughing.
It starts when Aunt Taryn
asks me to tell Grandma
dinner's ready. I knock on
my bedroom door.

Even with it closed, her scent—
some gag-me perfume,
combined with something
sharper—leaks into the hall.

No answer, so I coax,
"Hey, Grandma? Dinner."

> I'll be there when I get there.
> If you're in a huge hurry, go
> ahead and start without me.

I return to the kitchen.
"She said start without her."

> Aunt Taryn looks confused.
> Are you positive?

"That's what she said.
Maybe she's still tired."

Hannah helps Aunt Taryn put
big steaming bowls of leftover
Italian soup on the table.
I take a huge bite. "Yum.
It's even better tonight."

> *That's why I always make*
> *an extra-large pot.*
> *The longer the flavors*
> *blend, the better they taste.*

We are all savoring
the blend when Grandma
storms into the kitchen,
holding a glass half-filled
with clear liquid. Not water.

> *You couldn't wait five*
> *minutes?* she demands.

> Aunt Taryn drops her spoon.
> *Cal said you said to go ahead.*

Everyone looks at me, and
not in a good way.
"You did say to start."

Grandma parks her invisible
broomstick, joins us at the table.

*Apparently, the boy
is too stupid to recognize
sarcasm when he hears it.*

Mama, please! yelps Aunt Taryn.

I don't need her to defend me.
The s-word—*stupid*,
not *sarcasm*—has set off
explosions inside my head.

Sizzle!
      Pop!
            Bang!

I look the witch straight
in her wrinkled crone eyes.

"Maybe you should just say
what you mean. Otherwise,
people might think you have
Alzheimer's or something."

Cal! says Aunt Taryn.

Cal! says Uncle Bruce.

Hannah chokes on a laugh.

Are you calling me addled?
The old worm is seething.

I want to say *if the cauldron*
fits, but I'm pretty sure
that would make things worse.

"No. I don't think you're addled.
You know exactly what you're saying,
at least most of the time.

"Problem is, you don't care
if it hurts someone.
You're not crazy.
You're just mean."

I glance at the faces,
all focused on me.

Worried.
(Aunt Taryn.)

Irritated.
(Uncle Bruce.)

Semi-amused.
(Hannah.)

Blank.
(Grandma.)

I need a reaction.
I need to know she heard me.
I need to make her understand
that words can hurt.

"Oh, and our teacher told
us that things like intellect
are carried in our genes.
Which means if I'm stupid,
you must be, too."

FACT OR FICTION:
Everyone Looks Like I Zapped Them with a Stun Gun

Answer: I wish I had a camera.

No one says a word,
so I slurp soup and wait.

I'm the only one
with a spoon in my mouth.

I can't believe I said all
that. But it felt good
to finally confront her.

No, it felt great.
At least until she finally
settles on her comeback.

> *Perhaps I shouldn't have*
> *called you stupid.*
> *You are, however, insolent.*
> *I'd appreciate an apology.*

My head starts shaking
without me even telling it
to. "For what? Being alive?"

> *Cal, warns Uncle Bruce.*
> *You'd better quit now.*

He can probably see
my personal Hulk rising up
inside me, threatening
to bust right out of my skin.

I don't want to hold him back.
It hurts when I do.

And she isn't worth hurting for.

"Okay. I'm sorry.

"I'm sorry
my mom didn't live her life
the way you wanted her to.

"I'm sorry
you never forgave her.

"I'm sorry
you couldn't care
about me because
I'm related to my dad.

"I'm sorry
having dinner with you
makes me want to puke."

I push back from the table,
still hungry but not willing to stay.

As I leave, nervous chatter
fires up, and I hear
the Wicked Witch say,

The boy is a hothead.
Just like his father.

Oh, man.

Now I'm crying.

Quick.

Get away.

Don't let

anyone see.
Especially not her.

Crying means you're weak.

She has to think I'm strong.

I don't know

where to go.

Not my room.

It smells like her.

Not the bathroom.

Someone will need it.

Outside. Or garage.

No. Too cold.

So where?

Only one place
I can think of.

Hannah's room.

FACT OR FICTION:
Hannah Needs to Clean Under Her Bed

Answer: It's gross under here.

There's, like, dust.
Three dirty socks.
Hair scrunchie things.
Candy wrappers.
A water bottle.
And—yuck—a pair of undies.

I kick them off to one side,
along with two books,
one teen magazine
and a stuffed teddy
that's probably as old as Hannah.

But the bed frame is high.
There's space overhead
and air to breathe.
Better than a closet.
I could never hide
all closed up in there.

I burrow in.
 Listen to the floor
 creak under my back.
 Inhale the musty scent
 of old carpet
 and the bottom side
 of a mattress.

There are worse places
to be right now.
Like at the dinner table.

Definition of *Family Dynamics*:
How Family Members Deal with Each Other

After Cal leaves,
Mom and Dad and I
try not to talk about him.
Only Grandma wants to.

I wonder if it has anything
to do with what's in her glass.

> *You two are saints*
> *for moving that child in here.*
> *Too bad he can't appreciate it.*

> *Oh, I think he does, Mama.*
> *Cal's a pretty good kid,*
> *even though it might not*
> *always seem that way.*

> *His father is mentally ill.*
> *Have you had the boy tested?*

> *He had a whole battery*
> *of tests when he first got here,*
> says Dad. *Months of therapy, too.*

His therapist made us all
come in together a few times.
She talked about family
dynamics and how there
would be a long, hard period
of adjustment. She was right.

Maybe he needs more
sessions. Or different meds.
Something stronger, perhaps.

He isn't on medication,
Mom says. *His diagnosis*
didn't indicate a need.

Grandma snorts. *Maybe*
he needs a better therapist.
What was his diagnosis?

PTSD, offers Dad.

Post-traumatic stress
disorder? From what?

Mom shakes her head.
I'm sure you have some idea.
I mean, just think about it.
Meanwhile, please drop it.

Grandma starts to say
something, changes her mind.
She looks at Dad, then at me.

I shrug and finish my soup.
Even if I knew what Mom
meant, talking about Cal
behind his back feels wrong.

Grandma gives up. *I guess
you're right. What's on
the menu for tomorrow?*

Mom gives her the list:
        brined turkey
        stuffing with sausage
        mashed potatoes
        candied yams
        roasted cauliflower
        dinner rolls.

That's a lot of carbs, says
Grandma. *I should speed
walk in the morning.
Hope you have plenty of help.*

Guess she's not planning
on kitchen duty. I raise
my hand. "You've got me.
Give me something easy."

*A lot of the prep work
is already done . . .*

Mom starts talking about
the pie fillings—not pecan—
she's already put together,
and I tune out.

If a stranger peeked
in the window
right now, they'd think
our family dynamics
were working just fine.

It's like nothing bad even
happened a few minutes ago.
No drama. No arguments.

But Cal was mad. Hurt.
And I don't blame him,
even if maybe he started it.

Now that I'm thinking
about him, where did he go?

Another question:

                    Why
                    am
                    I
                    the
                    only
                    one
                    asking?

Definition of *Claustrophobia*:
Fear of Being in a Small Space

After promising Grandma
I'll be right back to show
her videos of my last
gymnastics meet, I excuse
myself and go see if I can find Cal.

He's not in the living room.
That would be too obvious.

I don't expect he'll be
in his own bedroom, but
I peek inside anyway.
Nope. Not there.

He's not in the bathroom,
either. And I'm sure
he won't be in my parents'
room, which leaves only
one other place to check.

It's dark in my bedroom,
and when I flip on the light,
it looks empty. But I've got
this feeling . . .

"Cal? Are you in here?"

Who wants to know?
His voice creeps out
from under my bed.

"I do. Are you playing
stalker again? Why
are you under there?"

> *I figured this would*
> *be the last place*
> *anyone would look.*

"It was, actually."

> *See? I'm not stupid.*

That really got to him.
"No one thinks you're
stupid, including Grandma."

> *Right. She thinks I'm insolent,*
> *but she's the one who's rude.*

"To be fair, you are rude
sometimes."

> *Figures you're on her side.*

"Cal, that was supposed
to be funny. Now please
come out from under my bed?"

> Okay. It's disgusting down
> here, anyway. Are you missing
> a teddy bear and some underwear?

My face gets all hot. "Leave
them there, okay?" He drags
himself out, and I ask,
"Wouldn't the garage
have been easier? Or a closet?"

> The garage is too cold.
> And closets give me
> claustrophobia. Plus
> they smell like dirty feet.

True. I'd rather not hang
out in one myself.

Definition of *Charity Case*:
Someone Others Help Out of Pity

"You should go finish
your dinner." Why am
I worried about that?

                    Nah. I lost my appetite.

Something Misty told me
once floats into my brain.
It was about a gymnastics
opponent, but it works here, too.

"If you let a rival get under
your skin, you give away
your power to that person."

                    Power? What power?

Spit sprays from his mouth.

                Kids don't have any power,
                but even if they did,
                I'd have less than you.

I can't believe how fast
he can flip from totally calm
to *screaming at the universe.*

"What do you mean?"

I. Have. No. Power.
Because I have nothing.
I'm a charity case.
Someone to feel sorry for.

No one cares about me,
except maybe Aunt Taryn,
and that's only because of Mom.

His words sink, heavy,
like stones in a pond.
I want to tell him he's wrong.
But I have to think for a minute.

"You know who else cares
about you? Mrs. Peabody
and Ms. C and Mr. Love."

No way. They only act like
they do because it's their job.

I concentrate harder.
Finally, it comes to me.
"Okay, then. Brylee.
She totally cares about you."

His face goes all red, but
at least he smiles. *Yeah.*
Maybe. She's pretty nice.

I remember how much
it bothered me the first time
Brylee stood up for Cal, and
now I don't get why.

He's still annoying.
He's still a fake kid.
He still makes me mad.

But I guess I'm getting
used to having him around.
Maybe I even care about him a little, too?

Definition of *Dilemma*:
A Problem with No Good Solution

Grandma's calling me
to come show her videos,
and that creates a dilemma.

I don't really want to leave
Cal alone here in my room.
Who knows what he might
get into—or shrink?

But there's no place else
for him to go, unless . . .
"You want to come watch
gymnastics with us?"

> *I'd rather eat a bowl of worms.*
> *Can I just stay here and read?*

"I guess . . ." I can't find
an excuse to say no. Oh.
Wait. "But you don't have
any books in here."

> *There's a teen magazine*
> *under the bed. Maybe I can*
> *learn all about hair chalk.*

I'm glad I don't have any.
My white sheets would
probably be rainbow-colored
by the time I got back.

"Okay, fine. Just please
don't mess with anything."

He points toward my bed.
The mess is under there.
I promise to leave it alone.

Mom already uploaded
all my videos—gymnastics
and dance—from her phone
to YouTube, and we watch
a few of them on Dad's laptop.

Grandma doesn't critique
the gymnastics, but
she picks on the dance.

Oh. You missed a step.
Too bad. Other than that,
it was a lovely routine.
Well, your frame could
have been straighter.

Not the worst comments,
and her voice isn't mean,
but she could've just said
good job. My feelings
are only a little hurt.

Still, I nod. "You're right."

Your mother was quite
the dancer, you know.
I thought she might take
it up professionally.

"But then she fell in love."

Grandma's shoulders sag
and she heaves a big sigh.

Oh, so you know the story.
Yes, but then she met
your father, and that was that.
It's a sad fact of life that
love too often kills passion.

Definition of *Passion*:
Strong Liking for Something; Deep Emotion

I'm not sure exactly
what Grandma meant.
I've heard people say
something they loved—
like dance—was their passion.

So, how can love kill passion?
Makes no sense, but whatever.
"I'm going to see if I can help
Mom with the prep work."

> *You're a sweet girl. I think*
> *I'll take a bath and go to bed.*

Grandma heads one way,
I go the other, but before
I can reach the kitchen,
loud whispers stop me
outside the door.

> Mom: *You choose* now *to tell*
> *me this? Thanksgiving?*

> Dad: *I'm sorry, Taryn.*
> *I didn't want to drop it on*
> *you, and I need to make plans.*

> Mom: *What is it you're not*
> *saying? Is there someone else?*

Dad: *No. I swear. I just need*
a little space for a while.

Space? No. He has to be
joking. Please, please.
Tell me he isn't leaving.

FACT OR FICTION:
No One Seems Thankful This Morning

Answer: Understatement.

I slept on the couch,
which wasn't so bad.
Except Aunt Taryn was up
really early, crashing
around in the kitchen.

And since the couch
isn't behind a closed door,
the noise woke me up
early, too. I lie here
for a few minutes,
listening to her work.

Eventually, guilt kicks in.
Someone should help her.
I fold up the blanket
I cocooned in last night,
stack the pillow on top.

Then I wander toward
the clatter, peek at the clock
on the wall. Six thirty-five.

I poke my head through
the door. "Do you always
start so early?"

Aunt Taryn jumps a little.
*Cal! Did I wake you? Sorry.
Yes. There's lots to do.*

Her voice sounds . . . sad.
She's probably just tired.

"Since I'm up, can I help?"

She doesn't quit moving—sink
to counter to cutting board—
but I can tell she's thinking.

Finally, she says, *Can you
chop celery and onions
without cutting off a finger?*

"Pretty sure I can
handle it. How small?"

Aunt Taryn gives a short
demonstration, then leaves
me to accomplish the task
while she rolls out pie crusts
and dumps in the fillings
she made yesterday.
She's quiet the whole time.

"Is everything okay?"
She usually has a lot
more to say. I figure
she'll tell me she's fine.

> Instead, she says, No,
> Cal, everything isn't okay.
> Bruce has decided he wants
> us to try living apart for a while.

FACT OR FICTION:
I Did Not Expect That

Answer: Not in a million years.

I mean, yes, they argue a lot.
But all parents do, right?
Of course, mostly
what I hear them
bickering about is me.

"It's my fault, isn't it?"

>   *Oh, Cal. You can't blame*
>   *yourself. It's complicated.*

I keep chopping but think
about all the times I heard
my name come up during
their arguments. It's me.

"Where's he going?"

She swallows hard and
I know she's trying not to cry.

>   *For now, he's moving in*
>   *with his parents. They only*
>   *live two hours away, so*
>   *he can still make at least*
>   *some of Hannah's activities.*

Hannah.

She's going to freak out.
And she'll totally blame me.
That's okay. She totally should.

Why did this have to
happen today?
Last year was my first
real Thanksgiving,
at least that I remember.

I guess Mom and Dad
and I might have done
the turkey and cranberry
sauce thing once or twice,
but I would've been really little.

After he went to prison,
Mom and I didn't have
much money, so maybe
we had chicken. Or meat loaf.

Then, when Dad
was released and moved
back in with us, every meal
was a nightmare.
None stands out
as decent, let alone
a celebration.

And once Mom got sick,
food was whatever
would stop my stomach
from growling.

So, yeah, I was looking
forward to another feast
like the one Aunt Taryn
put on the table last year.

But now it's pointless.

Grandma being here
already made everything
a little less happy.
This is terrible.

"How can you keep cooking?
You don't have to tell me,
but I'm a good listener."

> Aunt Taryn shrugs. *I want*
> *today to feel as*
> *normal as possible.*
> *Everything will change*
> *soon enough. Besides . . .*
>
> She struggles to smile.
> *What would we do with all*
> *this food if we didn't eat it?*

Donate it.
To a shelter.
Homeless people need
Thanksgiving, too.
I should know.
Homeless . . .

That's it.
I have to try and fix this.
The only way
I can think of
         is
             to
                 leave.

FACT OR FICTION:
This Time I'm Running Away

Answer: Definitely. I'm gone.

At least I will be
once Grandma is up
and out of my room.

While I'm waiting,
I keep helping in the kitchen.

Watching Aunt Taryn
lose herself in work,

    inhaling the scent
    of baking pies,

        soaking up the warmth
        of the oven—

            these things make me
            homesick before I'm gone.

How can I be homesick
if this isn't my home?

When did I start
to feel like it was,
or like I belong
with this temporary family?

A few words of one
of Mom's favorite songs
lift up inside me.
I can hear her crystal voice.

> *Don't it always seem to go*
> *that you don't know what*
> *you've got till it's gone?*

The thing is, Mom,
I lost everything
when I lost you.

It's good to feel safe,
and I've had that here.

But if that means
splitting up
this family,

I'll take my chances
on the outside,
as Dad used to say.

Yeah, he was talking
about being out
of prison after a long
time inside, and how
scary that seemed.

Which is weird, if you
think about it. How
could being free
scare you more
than being locked up?

FACT OR FICTION:
I Miss My Dad

Answer: Leave me alone.

Dad used to say: *There is no black
or white, only shades of gray.*

Yeah, and when it comes
to my dad, he's hard to talk about.

If black equals "bad"
and white equals "good,"
his shade of gray is charcoal,
with a couple of silver
streaks mixed in.

He was not good to Mom,
but after she was gone
he tried, for a little while,
to be good to me. He failed.

Life on the outside
(that includes me)
was too hard for him,
so that's why I'm here.

Scratch that. Why I *was* here.

> *Cal?* Aunt Taryn interrupts
> my thoughts. *Could you please
> help me with the turkey?*

I help her lift the heavy
bird out of the brining bucket
and into the sink, where
she rinses off the salty liquid.

"What time is dinner?"

> I usually aim for about
> two. As long as I get
> the turkey stuffed and
> into the oven by eight,
> that should be doable.

"You're an awesome cook.
You should go on one
of those TV shows."

I want to make her feel
better. Pretty sure
that wasn't enough.

Especially when we hear
Uncle Bruce's footsteps
headed this way,
followed by Hannah's
staccato chatter.

Aunt Taryn turns to me.
Don't say anything, okay?
Hannah doesn't know yet.

She should've known
before I did.

FACT OR FICTION:
Hannah Suspects

Answer: Yup.

You can tell by the way
she's babbling about stuff
that doesn't matter at all.

It's like she wants to make
sure no one says something
she doesn't want to hear.

Which means she probably
overheard a conversation
not meant for her ears.

Sometimes grown-ups forget
they're not the only people
in—or near—the room.

It's a kid's job to sneak
up on their parents, listen in.
Too bad surprises aren't always good.

But that was totally wrong.
If a kid's parents are breaking
up, they should tell her right away.

Guess Aunt Taryn needed
to blow off steam this morning.
That's why she confided in me.

Don't worry, Hannah.
From now on, you'll always
be the first to know.

Definition of *Divert*:
Make Something Change Direction

I follow Dad to the kitchen,
where Mom and Cal
have been cooking for a while,
from how things look.

I had a hard time sleeping
last night, and I guess
it shows, because Cal says,

> *Whoa. Those are some*
> *heavy-duty dark circles*
> *under your eyes.*

Figures he'd be the one
who noticed. Mom and
Dad? Not at all, at least
not until he mentioned it.

> *Rough night?* asks Dad.

The worst, not that I'll admit
it. I kept stressing about
what Dad meant when
he said he needed some space.
I must've misunderstood, though,
because he and Mom seem fine.

Just in case, I'll keep talking,
divert the conversation
so nothing like my parents
splitting up is mentioned.

"Guess I was excited
about today." Lame.

"Are we having cranberry
sauce?" Lamer. We always
have cranberry sauce.

Hannah, are you okay?
asks Mom. *Did you think
I'd forget how much you love
cranberry sauce?*

See? Cranberry sauce.
Because I love it.
Everything is normal.
Just as it should be.

Dad pours a cup of coffee.
*Anyone up for the Macy's
parade? It should start soon.*

"Me! Me!" I'll stick close
by his side so he knows
how important he is to me.

Mom says she still has work
to do, and Cal chooses to stay
with her in the kitchen.
Okay by me. Less chance
of Dad getting upset.

The parade is rad.
I love the huge balloons
and fancy floats, and I'm glad
we can watch it on TV.
It looks really cold
in New York City.

Still, it's a place I want
to visit. "Will you take me
there someday, Dad?"

> *To New York? I'd like to.*
> *I thought about moving there*
> *once, a long time ago.*

"Before you met Mom?"

> *No, actually, it was after.*
> *I had a chance at a great job*
> *in Manhattan. But I couldn't*
> *convince her to go.*

"Why not?"

> *She said it was too expensive*
> *to live there, and she was right.*
> *Plus, she wanted me to finish*
> *college, and she was right*
> *about that, too.*

"Mom's always right."

He's quiet for a long time.
Finally, he says, *It seems like
Mom's always right. Once
in a while, she's wrong.*

He doesn't say more,
but suddenly I feel the need
to divert the conversation
again. "Look at that Captain
Marvel balloon! She's rad!"

*Yes, she is. The world needs
more girl superheroes.*

"I think there are lots.
You just can't see them
because they hide in plain sight."

Like in the kitchen.

Definition of *Backfire*:
Go All Wrong

Dad doesn't agree or disagree.
In fact, he just goes quiet.
I'm not even sure he's still
paying attention to the TV.

All I wanted to do
was make him feel happy
to be here, at home
with Mom and me
and maybe even Cal.

I think my plan backfired.

About halfway through
the parade, the delish
smell of roasting turkey
drifts from the kitchen,
and I can hear Mom
and Cal's muffled voices.

Talking. About what exactly,
I don't know, but they're
not arguing or yelling.

How can that not make
Dad content? Instead,
he seems anxious.

And now Grandma appears,
wearing a fancy jade-green
warm-up suit embroidered
with her initials.

> *Is that the Macy's parade?*
> *You know, Macy's stock*
> *has tanked recently.*

Adults sure know how
to make fun stuff boring.
Dad and Grandma spend
way too long yakking
about the stock market,
whatever that is.

I concentrate on the TV
until Grandma finally goes
speed walking to burn off
calories she hasn't eaten yet.
Honestly, she looks pretty good
for a grandma, so I guess
the exercise is working.

No workouts for me today,
though. I'm hanging with Dad.
Except now he says,

> *I'll be right back. I need*
> *to make a phone call.*

"On Thanksgiving?"

> *I promised my parents*
> *I'd give them a ring.*

"Gram and GrandpaL?"
That's my funny name
for Grandpa L(incoln).
"Can I talk to them, too?"

> He hesitates, but now says,
> *Sure. I've got something*
> *important to discuss first,*
> *then I'll put you on to say hi.*

I don't like how that sounds,
but all I can do is say, "Okay."

Definition of *Disintegrate*:
Fall Apart

Whatever it is Dad wants
to say in private to Gram
and GrandpaL takes ten minutes.

He keeps his promise
and brings me the phone
after that. We put it on speaker.

> *Tell us all about school.*

I do. I even tell them
about the family tree.

> *Tell us all about gymnastics.*

I do. I explain how I'm this
close to leveling up.

> *Tell us all about dance.*

I do. And I invite them
to my next recital.

> *We'll see if we can work
> it out. We need to spend
> more time together.*

We should, and that's
exactly what I say.

But it will take more than
words to make it happen.

Still, it's good to talk
to them. Right up until
GrandpaL says to Dad,

>   *So, what time should we*
>   *expect you on Sunday, son?*

With that one little question,

                        my life
        begins to
                    disintegrate.

Dad's expression
says he
did not
expect
to answer
that
in
front
of
me.

But he has to.

>   *Early afternoon.*

When he hangs up,
I ask, "Why
are you going there?"

> He swallows hard.
> *I'm staying with them*
> *for a while.*

"How long?"

> *I'm not sure, Hannah.*

"But why? Don't you
love us anymore?"

> *I will always love you,*
> *no matter what. And I'll*
> *always take care of you.*

Definition of *Indigestion*:
Stomachache

I haven't eaten a thing
since dinner last night.

But suddenly my stomach
aches, churning hot acid.
How can words give
you indigestion?

I ask straight-out, "Are you
and Mom getting divorced?"

> *No. We just need to spend
> a little time apart.*

"How little is 'little'?"

> *I wish I could tell you.
> But I won't be that far away.
> I'll still see you lots.*

My eyes sting. "It's not
the same thing! You belong
here. With us. Please, Dad."

He doesn't answer, just
gets up and goes down
the hall to his bedroom.

Now all those familiar
holiday smells fill the house.
Tears brim my eyes
and streak down my cheeks.

How can Mom cook like this
is any other Thanksgiving?

How can Mom act like
everything is normal?

I go to the kitchen to make
sure she knows Dad plans
to leave us on Sunday.

She's alone there,
standing at the window,
looking at something—
or maybe nothing at all.

"Mom? Why didn't you tell
me Dad's moving out?"

>She turns. Slowly. *Oh,*
Hannah. I didn't know
myself until yesterday.
He sprung it on me, too.

"But, what . . . I mean,
how . . . what's going to
happen to us without him?"

> *Nothing will change for*
> *now. I mean, other than*
> *he won't be living here.*

"Do you want him to go?"

> *Of course not! This is not*
> *my decision. But maybe*
> *he'll decide he'd rather be with us.*

We hear Grandma come
through the front door,
back from her walk.

> *Don't say anything in front*
> *of your grandmother, please.*
> *She'll find out soon enough.*

Definition of *Best-Laid Plans*:
Something That Doesn't Work Out as Expected

But Grandma finds out
right away. Not because
of something I say, though.

A few minutes after she gets
back from her walk, she comes
into the kitchen, holding a note.

> *I found this on Cal's pillow.*
> *You'd better take a look.*

She hands it to Mom.
It only takes her a couple
of seconds to read it.

> *Oh, no. He can't have been*
> *gone very long. You didn't*
> *see him on your walk?*

> Grandma shakes her head.
> *No. I mean, I wasn't looking*
> *for him, and if he went the other*
> *direction, I wouldn't have seen*
> *him.*

> *Hannah, get on your bike*
> *and ride a few blocks. See if*
> *you can spot Cal. He ran away.*

"What do I say if I do see him?"

Tell him to please come
back so we can talk it over.
And that I said this most
definitely is not his fault.

Now Grandma knows for sure.
As Mom might say, the best-laid
plans don't always work out.

FACT OR FICTION:
I Have No Clue Where I'm Going

Answer: That is a fact.

I didn't have much time.
Just enough to throw a few
clothes into my backpack
and scribble a goodbye note.

This is what it said:

> Thank you for taking care
> of me. I know it's been hard,
> especially for Uncle Bruce.
>
> I also know I'm the reason
> for him wanting to leave.
> That is not okay, so I'll go
> instead. Don't worry about
> me. I'm a survivor. Love, Cal.

I left it on my pillow and . . .
Wait. Oh, no. Grandma
will probably see it first.
That wasn't a great plan.

Speaking of plans, now that
I'm out of the house, I realize
I should've planned better.
Okay, I should've planned.

Period.

At least I grabbed my jacket.
It's gray and cold out here,
and it's barely noon.
If I have to sleep outside . . .

Yes, I've slept on the street
before, in a busy city
with plenty of places
to snug up against buildings.

I can't do anything about
the cold, but I could maybe find
a sheltered spot that might
work for a little while.

But this is a small town.
A kid smooshed into
the warmest corner
he can claim might not
make the news Day One.

But by the third or fourth,
pretty sure someone
will notice and start
asking questions.

I brought all the allowance
I've saved. Around seventy
dollars. That will buy
a bus ticket to somewhere.

But there are a couple
of problems with that.

One: Can a kid on his own
                    buy a bus ticket?
Two: Even if he can,
                    where would he buy it to?

FACT OR FICTION:
My Stomach Prefers to Be Empty

Answer: Never.

But it isn't something
I've had to worry about
since I've been living
with Aunt Taryn.

Wandering the sidewalk,
the smell of food is everywhere.
Almost every window and door
leaks Thanksgiving reminders,
and now I'm starving.

I didn't have breakfast.
Another thing I could've
planned better. Yes,
I could duck into some
little convenience store
determined to stay open
despite it being a holiday.

But
A) I don't want to spend
any money just yet

and
B) a Slim Jim and a Snickers
bar won't cut it today

          and
C) I think I know where I can
share a Thanksgiving table.

I've been there before
a few times—not to eat,
but to show people where it is.

Once in a while, when I'm on
one of my cool-off roams,
I come across someone
new to living on the street.

If you're homeless for the first
time, you don't always know
where you can find help.

I learned about the soup
kitchen from the shelter
in town where I go sometimes
to hang out with the children.

When Mom and I stayed
in the shelter that time,
there wasn't much for a kid
to do, and it would have been nice
to have someone to play with.

So when I happen to pass
by the local place, I go in
to see if there are kids
inside who feel the same way.

Sometimes there are,
sometimes there aren't,
but it never hurts to check.
Every kid deserves a friend.

FACT OR FICTION:
You Can Eat for Free at a Soup Kitchen

Answer: Yes, at most of them.

A soup kitchen is a dining
room where people in need
can eat at least one meal
a day. Usually for free.

By the time I reach this one,
there's a really long line.
I tap the guy in front of me.
"What time do they open?"

I barely touched him, but
I guess it made him nervous,
because he goes all stiff.
But when he turns, the look
in his eyes changes instantly
from suspicion to sympathy.

> *The doors open at noon.*
> *You here all alone?*

"Yeah. My dad isn't feeling
so good." The lie comes easily.

> *Oh. Okay. We've got about*
> *twenty minutes. You hungry?*
> *When was the last time you ate?*

"Yesterday. I'm hungry
but I'm doing okay."

*Good to hear. I hate
to see young'uns in trouble.*

There are lots of kind people
in the world. Some are homeless.

While we wait, I check out
the line. It's mostly men,
all ages, all colors, all sizes.
Some could use warmer clothes.
I wish I had some to spare.

There are several women,
too, including a couple
who look like teenagers.
Runaways like me, I guess.
Or maybe their parents
kicked them out. It happens.

One lady is holding a baby.
Beside her, a little girl,
about two, clutches the hem
of her mama's jacket
with one hand, sucks
the thumb on the other.

Every person has a story,
a reason for being here
today. I'd like to know
what some of them are.

But if I asked someone
to tell me theirs,
they'd probably want
me to tell them mine.

FACT OR FICTION:
The Food Here Is Good

Answer: We'll find out soon.

Finally, someone inside
comes to unlock the door,
and when it opens,
the line begins
a slow shuffle forward.

I'm near the end,
so it takes a while
for me to feel the heat
escaping the building
and smell the feast,
which turns out
to be pretty good,
especially considering

a lot of the people
who cooked and are
serving it are volunteers

who could be home
feasting in private
with their own families.

The service is cafeteria
style. I grab a tray.

So many choices!
Turkey.   Ham.
Stuffing.   Mac 'n' cheese.
Green beans.   Corn.
Cranberry sauce: jellied, whole berry.
Potatoes: mashed, scalloped, sweet.

I'm pointing to my pie
selection (apple—not big
on pumpkin) when a familiar
voice falls into my ear.

      Cal? What are you doing here?

I spin. "Brylee? What
are *you* doing here?"

      *Volunteering. My church
      is sponsoring this dinner.*

How fast can I make
up an excuse?

      Why aren't you home?

Not fast enough.
I pick up my tray.

"Come on. Let's sit down."

Brylee follows me over
to a table at the very
back of the big room.

We find two seats, and
I think what to say.

What's going on, Cal?

I open my mouth,
but no words spill out.
That says a lot.

It's okay. You can tell me.

Suddenly, I want to.
I start with Grandma,
move all the way through
my time under Hannah's bed
and finish up with the news
about Aunt Taryn and Uncle Bruce.

"It's totally on me that
they're splitting up.
Uncle Bruce never wanted
me there. It's why he's been
spending so much time away."

She tsk-tsks. *It's not fair*
to blame yourself. I did that
when my parents broke up, but
now I know it wasn't my fault.

"Thanks, Brylee."
That was sweet.
But she isn't me.

FACT OR FICTION:
Brylee Is Really My Friend

Answer: I think she is.

I look at her and realize
she's one of the few
people who've ever taken
the time to get to know me.

If I run away, I'll miss her.
And, believe it or not,
I'll miss school. I never
thought I'd feel that way.

But I don't know how
to reverse course now,
so I'll just change
the subject. "You want
to talk about your parents?"

> *Maybe later. I'm supposed
> to be helping in the kitchen.
> Eat your dinner. But please
> go home after, okay?*

"I'll think about it."
As she starts away, I put
my hand on her arm.
"Hey, Brylee? Thanks again."

> When she smiles, her face
> lights up. *No problem.*

I tell myself to ask her
about her parents sometime.
Does that mean I think
I'll have that chance?

I still don't know where
I'll go after I finish dinner.
Brylee made me kind of
homesick again.

But with Uncle Bruce leaving,
home will be different.

As I think about that,
a whole new worry
pops into my head.

We're supposed to go
to court soon.
What will the judge
think about custody
if Uncle Bruce isn't there?

And suddenly it hits me
that if he and Aunt Taryn
don't know where to find me,

Dad can't, either.

Definition of *Prejudiced*:
Narrow-Minded

No matter what happens
tomorrow or next week
or next year, I'll always
remember this Thanksgiving.

And not in a good way.

When Mom asked me to
ride my bike and go look
for Cal, I did. But I didn't
go very far or look very hard.

Because this *is* his fault.

Mom swears it's not,
that she and Dad started
having problems way
before Cal moved in.

Maybe that's the truth.

But if there were tiny cracks
in their marriage before,
when Cal came, he wedged
them bigger. Wider. Deeper.

Now they're canyons.

Grandma says love is not
supposed to last, that
"ever after" is a fantasy.
But she is prejudiced.

Because her own love died.

That's what Mom told me.
And I believe her.

Definition of *On Pins and Needles*:
Nervously Waiting for Something

All of us have been on pins
and needles, waiting to see
if Cal really left for good.

> *He'll be back*, Grandma
> insists. *He'll be back.*

> *Give him until dark.*
> Dad's usual advice.
> *He's always home by dinner.*

> *I planned dinner for two,*
> argues Mom. *Not near dark.*
> *Besides, this is different.*
> *He's never said goodbye before.*

Mom's pretty smart.
I think it's different
this time, too. His note
sounded serious,
like for once he meant
exactly what he said.

Part of me
wants him gone.

Another part wonders
where he'll end up.

Not to mention
what awful things
might happen to him there.
I read books. I watch movies.
I know bad stuff happens
to kids, especially runaways.

Mom leaves Grandma
in charge of basting
the turkey while she drives
around, searching for Cal.

                    Dad distracts himself
                    with a football game.

Mom returns, disappointed.
Keeps working on dinner.
But I know her worry meter
is spinning like crazy.
I can see her brain working
in the way she peels potatoes
and chops cauliflower.

One word comes to mind:
                    maniacally.
Definition:
                    like a crazy person.

In between tasks, she paces.
Goes to a door.
Looks out.
Goes to a different door.
Looks out.

Ditto any window
facing the street.

Finally, she decides,

> *I'm calling the police.*

I'm the only one who says
anything. "Yeah, you should."

She doesn't want to dial 9-1-1,
and it takes a while to connect
with a live nonemergency
person. The conversation,
as I can hear it, goes like this:

Something muffled on
the other end.

> Mom: *He's twelve.*

—

> *I'm his aunt and legal guardian.*

Nothing like this.

—

There was some upset this morning.

—

No friends that I know of.

—

Would you just, please, send someone?

Her voice now is frantic.
I guess it works, because
they're sending an officer.

When they can.
It's a holiday.

I thought police officers
were supposed to care.

Oh, wait. A little while ago,
I didn't care so much myself.

Definition of *Savory*:
Spicy; Flavorful

Our holiday meal is on
the table before anyone
shows up at the door.

The turkey's roasted perfectly,
the stuffing is savory and
there's plenty of gravy for the potatoes.

Mom skipped the rolls,
but melted extra butter
and cheese on the cauliflower.

The cranberry sauce is sweet-tart,
the yams hidden beneath marshmallow
clouds, but only Grandma's hungry.

At first no one talks.
It's so quiet, you can hear
chewing. Cal's on our minds.

But I wonder if anyone
else worries that this might
be our last Thanksgiving together.

> Finally, Dad says to Mom,
> *I'm not so sure calling*
> *the police was the best idea.*

I couldn't take a chance
on him disappearing. He's been
through so much and come so far.

> *You had to do something,*
> says Grandma. *But the child*
> *is an actor, and this is all a show.*

I hope she's right. Not so long
ago, I would've thought so
for sure. Now I don't know.

We're still picking at our plates
when the doorbell rings.

> *I'll get it,* says Mom. *Stay here.*

She returns, trailed by Officer Ash,
who's probably the tiniest
policeman—woman—ever.

While Mom goes to get Cal's
goodbye letter, Officer Ash
asks a few questions.

> *What was he wearing?*
> *Is anything missing?*
> *Where does he hang out?*

Mom comes back with the note
and Cal's most recent
school picture.

> Officer Ash checks out the photo
> and says, *Hey, I've seen this kid
> before. Oh . . . where was it?*

Dad and I exchange looks
that mean, *What did Cal do
that we don't know about?*

> But Mom only says, *I think
> he's wearing his Cubs jacket.
> It's his favorite, and it's gone.*

> *Good to know*, says the police
> lady. *Well, I'll definitely keep
> an eye out. One question . . .*

Definition of *Motive*:
Reason for Doing Something

Officer Ash asks what Mom
and Dad want her to do
with Cal if she locates him.

> Grandma jumps in. *Take*
> *him in to juvenile hall.*
> *Show him what it's like.*
> *Otherwise he'll end up*
> *a vicious lout, like his father.*

I glance at Dad, but before
he can answer, Mom speaks up.

> *I think it's important*
> *to remember his motive.*
> *He was trying to save*
> *our marriage, not hurt us.*

It's hard to argue with that,
and Dad doesn't even try.
He shrugs an okay.

> *If you find him, please*
> *bring him home. Tell him*
> *we love him very much.*

The police lady nods and
explains it's best not to involve
the courts except as a last resort.

Once he's in the system, you
lose control. Here's my card,
with my direct number.
Call if you hear something
or if he comes home on his own.

Officer Ash has been gone
maybe twenty minutes
when the phone rings.

I answer. "Oh, hey, Brylee.
Happy Thanksgiving. What's up? . . .
Really? Okay, thanks."
Wow. What a coincidence.

"Hey, Mom, Dad. Guess
where Cal is, or at least where
he was a little while ago."

Mom puts in a call
to Officer Ash, but has to
leave a voice message.

       I'll go see if I can spot Cal,
       Mom decides.

But just as she's getting
ready to walk out the door,
the police lady calls back.
Mom puts her on speakerphone.

I've got him in my car.
I was cruising downtown
and happened to spot
a cute kid in a Cubs jacket.
He says he was walking
toward home, by the way.

> *Well, good,* says Grandma.
> *This calls for a celebration.*
> *How about some pie?*

I don't get it. I thought
she wanted him to go
to juvenile hall.
Adults are weird.

Definition of *Sarcastic*:
Snarky; Saying One Thing, Meaning Another

Grandma was serious
about having pie,
but I guess she didn't mean
it was supposed to be
a celebration because

> Mom says, *Must you always*
> *be so sarcastic, Mama?*

> *Who, me? Sarcastic? We're*
> *happy he's coming home,*
> *aren't we? Pecan or pumpkin?*

> *Should we clear the table*
> *or see if Cal wants to eat?*

"Uh, Mom. He was at the soup
kitchen, remember? Brylee
said he had dinner there."

> *But what if it wasn't good?*
> *What if he's still hungry?*

> *Stop it, Taryn,* snaps Dad.
> *Don't coddle the kid. If*
> *he's hungry, there are plenty*
> *of leftovers. He can snack later.*

Guess Dad's still mad
at Cal. He excuses himself
and goes in search of
another football game.

That leaves Mom and me
to put away the food
while Grandma picks
pecans out of her pie.

She piles them on one
side of her plate, scrapes
the gooey stuff off the crust
and eats it. Very slowly.

"Why did you make pecan
pie if you don't like pecans?"

Who says I don't like them?

Goopy stuff gone,
she pops the nuts
into her mouth

one
by
one,

like they're candy.

I watch her chew
each pecan and swallow
it before eating
the next one.

She reminds me
of me, sort of.
Cool.
In control.

At least I'm like that
most of the time.
Or, was like that.

Before today,
only Cal could throw
me off rhythm.
But now, with Dad
leaving, I feel like
I'm in a little boat,
and all the weight
is on one side.

Will it flip and sink?

FACT OR FICTION:
Riding in a Cop Car Rocks

Answer: As long as you're up front.

I really was heading home.
As I left the soup kitchen,
Brylee said something
that made me think.

> *If your uncle is moving out,*
> *don't you think your aunt*
> *might need your help?*

Boom. True. Aunt Taryn
has helped me a lot.
I should be there for her.

There I was, walking pretty fast,
when this patrol car came cruising
up behind me. I didn't notice until
it slowed way down and coasted.

My first thought was *uh-oh.*
I've had more than one
bad experience with cops.
So when the window went
down, I almost took off.

But then the officer said,
Hey, Cal. Let me take you
home, okay? Everyone's worried.
Oh, and your aunt said to
tell you she loves you.

That stopped me cold.
Because here's the thing.

The last person who told me
she loved me was my mom,
and she died an hour later.

I guess I knew Aunt Taryn
cared, but I never thought
about it like love.

"Do you want me to ride
in back?" I asked Officer Ash.

> *Oh, no. If you have a choice,*
> *never opt for the back seat*
> *of a patrol car. Things get*
> *gross back there pretty often.*

"You mean, like, blood?"

First, I imagined gunshot wounds,
but then I remembered it would
probably be the guy with the gun
in back, not the guy with the wound.

> That's one thing, yes. You'll
> have to guess about the rest.
> But sometimes people need
> to use the bathroom and can't.

Yeah, the front seat
sounded a lot better.

FACT OR FICTION:
Officer Ash Recognizes Me

Answer: It takes her a while.

When I get in the car, I ask
if we can turn on the siren.
She says sorry, no way, unless
it's an actual emergency.

But once we're off the main
drag, she lets me turn on the lights.
For a few seconds. And now
she's asking all kinds of questions.

> *How's school? You like it?*

"It's okay. Better than most."

> *Everything good at home?*

"Obviously not, or I wouldn't
be here on Thanksgiving."

> *Valid point. Hey, how did you*
> *know about the soup kitchen?*

"From the shelter. I hang
out there sometimes."

> *In case you need a place?*

"Nah. I play with the little
kids. They deserve friends."

You do that on your own?

"Yeah. Once I had to sta—"

*That's it! That's where
I've seen you before.*

She tells me this story:

*Once, I brought in a young mom.
She was struggling with intake,
and her children were so scared.
It was hard. You were playing
a game with another kid and
asked if they wanted to join in.*

"Oh, yeah. I remember.
Two little girls."

She nods. *That's right. Not
a lot of kids would bother
taking the time to hang out
with disadvantaged children.*

You're a decent young man.
So do me a favor and stay
out of trouble. That includes
running away. Once you're in
the system, you're stuck there.

"I know. My uncle got locked
up when he was in high school.
He spent a lot of time in juvie,
and later he went to prison."

The uncle I just met?

"Oh, no. Not Uncle Bruce.
My dad's brother, Frank."
I don't like thinking about
him and I sure don't want
to talk any more about him.

Luckily, I don't have to.

Listen. I read the note you left.
If you haven't already heard
this, you must understand that
couples split up all the time
and kids too often blame themselves.

"That's what my friend Brylee
told me. She also said Aunt Taryn
will need my help even more."

Brylee sounds like a smart
girl. Listen to your friend.
Oh, man. Hold on a minute.

There's some kind of trouble
up ahead on the sidewalk.
Two big guys are double-teaming
against a smaller dude.

Officer Ash whips against the curb,
keys her radio and calls for backup.

Stay put. And don't touch
anything. Nothing. Promise?

FACT OR FICTION:
Officer Ash Is Scary

Answer: She doesn't scare me.

But when she gets out and asks
the big guys what they're doing,
they back off right away.

Maybe it's her voice.
Maybe it's her badge.
Maybe it's her gun.

Whatever, it's awesome.
The top of her head barely
reaches the height of the biggest
dude's shoulders, but he looks
totally freaked out.

Still, I'm glad when another
squad car pulls up. In fact,
I didn't realize it, but I was
holding my breath, worried for her.

Officer Ash talks to the little guy
for a few, and the other cop takes
the big men's IDs. Now he speaks
into his radio. Bet he's checking
for warrants, like in the movies.

And now one more cruiser joins
the action. So we can leave.

Sorry about that, but I'm glad

we came along when we did.
That poor man was in trouble.

I don't get to see what
happens to the bad guys,
but I'm guessing they wish
we wouldn't have come along.

As we start toward home
again, I ask, "Do you ever
get scared, doing your job?"

> *Once in a while. But I knew*
> *there would be risks involved*
> *and I'm cautious by nature.*
> *Why? You thinking about*
> *being a policeman one day?*

That makes me laugh.
"Probably not the best job
for me. I am *not* cautious
by nature. I might write
stories about them, though."

> *She grins. Well, if you ever*
> *need an interview, you know*
> *who to call. Meanwhile,*
> *don't forget—people need you.*

> *Your aunt, kids at the shelter.*
> *Keep shining your light.*

FACT OR FICTION:
My Mom Also Told Me That

Answer:

If I said yes,
you wouldn't believe
                        it

and you'd say this
paper-thin memory
                        is

something I invented.
But those words rise
                        like

the moon—soft and low.
They make me feel as if
                        she's

alive in my heart,
believing in me like she
                        always

did, whispering
praise, lifting me
                        with

her presence and
insisting she wants
                        me

to have a real home.

FACT OR FICTION:
I'm Relieved to Be Home

Answer: Yes and no.

Officer Ash escorts me
to the door. We go inside,
where it's warm and smells
like turkey. Uncle Bruce
is watching a game,
but he stands and says,

> *Thanks for bringing him*
> *home. No trouble, I take it?*

> *None at all. Cal's a good*
> *kid. I think he'll be just fine.*

She doesn't offer details,
and Uncle Bruce doesn't ask
for them. Probably thinks
she says that stuff about
every runaway she brings home.

"Can I give you a hug?" I ask her.
Weird. I'm not the hugging type.

> *You may. Then I should go.*

It's a nice hug, and before
she deserts me, she says,

> *You've got this.*

Once she's gone, I don't feel
very brave. I can tell Uncle
Bruce is mad, because
he doesn't even look at me.

Doesn't matter. I should
say something. "I'm sorry."

> Really. For what exactly?

"For running away and making
everyone worry. For messing up
Thanksgiving, not to mention
your life. I can't change anything
now. All I can do is try to be better."

I expect him to yell or
ignore me, so I'm surprised
when he calmly says,

> Apology accepted. Go let
> Taryn know you're home.

"Okay." I nod toward
the TV. "Who's playing?"

> Detroit and Chicago.

The Lions and the Bears.
"Ooh. Can I watch?"
I'm sure he'll say no TV
for the rest of my life.

Instead: *I guess so.*

Definition of *Contrite*:
Very, Very Sorry

Mom and I have all the leftovers
put away and are working
on the giant pile of dishes
when Cal comes into the kitchen.

> *Hi. I'm back. Can I help*
> *you do anything?*

>> *You can never take off like that*
>> *again,* says Mom. *Want food?*

> *No, I'm not hungry. I ate.*

"Bet it wasn't as good
as Mom's." Even if hardly
anyone touched the food.

> *Yeah. I'm very, very sorry.*

"Hey. Did you really get
to ride in a police car?"

>> His face lights up. *Uh-huh.*
>> *It was so cool. I got shotgun,*
>> *which doesn't mean I got*
>> *to touch the shotgun. But*
>> *I did get to turn on the lights.*

And guess what. We came
across a couple of bad guys
trying to rob this little dude.
Officer Ash pulled over real fast
and told me to call for backup—

"Cal . . ."

Seriously. It was a 10-78.
Officer needs assistance.
She figured if she put me
in charge of the radio,
I'd leave the shotgun alone.

But you should've seen her.
She's teeny, you know, and
when she went after those
giant guys, they freaked.

The hugest one mouthed
off, and I thought he might
come at her, so I jumped out
and yelled, "Backup's two
minutes away." It was more
like five, but they didn't
know that, and that gave
the victim time to split.

His story almost sounds
believable. Almost.

> Two more squad cars got
> there and those cops checked
> for warrants. They must've found
> something, because they handcuffed
> the bad guys and hauled them to jail—

> > That's where you should
> > be right now, interrupts
> > Grandma, who kind of
> > appears out of nowhere.

How contrite is Cal?
Guess we'll find out.

Definition of *Embellish*:
Invent Details to Make a Story More Interesting

Cal studies Grandma
for a few seconds,
deciding how to react.
He must notice the glass
in her hand, which keeps
refilling itself, or so it seems.

Everyone knows what
she's drinking is some
kind of alcohol. Mom and
Dad hardly ever drink,
so the smell is obvious,
even clear across the kitchen.

Cal could leap on that.
Instead, he says,

> *Maybe you're right, and I should*
> *be in jail, but I'm glad to have another*
> *chance. Aunt Taryn, I know you'll need*
> *extra help now, so tell me what I can do.*

I think Grandma wanted
to fight. Her mouth falls
open and stays that way,
like it can't figure out
how to form words.

It's Mom who speaks up.
Thank you, Cal. I appreciate
your offer and will take you
up on it soon, I'm sure.

Well, if you don't need me
right now, Uncle Bruce said
I can watch the football game.

Now *my* jaw drops.
"You're kidding, right?"
I figured he'd ground Cal
for weeks. Is he totally going to
quit doing the parent thing?

Cal shrugs. *He said okay.*

As he starts to leave,
I have to ask, "Hey, Cal.
You made up all that stuff
about the cops and bad guys,
right?" No one could get
that lucky, seeing something
like that for real.

Nope. Most of it went down
just like that, though I might
have embellished the facts
a little. Creating drama
is what I do best, you know.

That's for sure, but
I'm starting to wonder
if it's always on purpose.

What comes first?
Drama?
Or Cal?

> After he's gone, Grandma
> says, *Without consequences,*
> *the boy's antics will continue.*
> *No punishment at all?*

I think he's been punished
enough, Mama. Let's salvage
what we can of this day.

Definition of *Salvage*:
Save; Reclaim

Rather than try to save
anything, Grandma goes
to take a nap, claiming
L-tryptophan fatigue.

That's whatever it is in
turkey that makes you sleepy.
I think there was at least
one other thing that made
her feel that way.

Mom's starting the dishwasher
when I say, "I'm not sure
how to ask this except just
to do it, so . . . Is Grandma okay?"

What do you mean?

"I mean, does she always
drink that stuff?"

Mom's sigh is massive.
*I suppose it was naïve to
believe you wouldn't notice.
But since you have, we need
to talk. Come on. Let's sit.*

She asks what I know
about alcoholism and I
have to answer, "Not very
much, except sometimes
people die from it."

That's because it's a disease.
Sort of like diabetes. It can
be treated, but treatment
doesn't always work.

"If it's a disease, does that
mean you can catch it?"

No. But you can inherit it.
Yes, my mom has the disease,
so I could develop it, too, which
is why I don't drink very often.

"So, it's carried in our genes,
like we learned in school.
And I could have it, too?"

That's right. Or maybe not.
It isn't always passed down.
But when you're old enough
to decide whether or not
to drink, choose carefully.

I think it over for a minute
or two. "If it can be treated,
why doesn't Grandma go
to the doctor? She could die."

It's complicated. Mom never
got over what happened between
my sister and her, and when
Caryn passed away without them
reconciling, she was devastated.

Drinking can't change that,
but it can make her forget
how sad and lonely she is,
at least temporarily. You have
to want help to seek treatment.

She doesn't want help.
But does she want to die?

Definition of *Heart-to-Heart*:
Honest

I'm glad Mom and I had
a heart-to-heart talk
about Grandma.

It gives me something
to think about besides
Dad leaving on Sunday.

It's hard to hold it all
inside, but by the next morning,
I know what I have to do.

I don't say a word
to Grandma, but I try
to keep her company
so she won't feel lonely.

I even go on a not-so-
speedy walk with her.
It's more like a stroll,
but if it works for her, okay.

"Do you exercise every day?"

> *I do my best. It's a good*
> *habit, and good habits*
> *help make up for bad ones.*

It's like she invited me to ask,
"You have bad habits?"

One or two. Who doesn't?

But she doesn't say
anything more about it,
closing the door again.
On the way home, we talk
about school and the weather.

When we get back,
Dad's into paperwork (or packing).
Mom's doing laundry.
Cal's reading, of course.

Grandma disappears
into the bedroom.
She won't start drinking
this early, will she?

But I'm afraid that's exactly
what she has in mind.
I need to talk to somebody.

"Hey, Cal. Want to ride bikes?"

He looks up from his book
suspiciously. Can't blame him.
It's the first time I've ever asked.

Uh . . . I guess so?

I don't give him time to change
his mind. I let Mom know
what we're doing and head
to the garage. Cal grabs his jacket.

I jump on my bike, pedal straight
down the block and around
the corner to the park, stop
at a table in the sun.

> Cal's right behind me.
> *That was a short ride.*

"Uh-huh. I wanted to talk
to you, but not where
anyone could hear . . ."

> *You're mad about Uncle Bruce.*

"No. I mean, yeah, I hate
it. What if they get a divorce?"

> *There are worse things.*

"Not to me! It's the same
as losing your . . ." But
it's not. I swallow hard.
"Sorry. It's not even close."

No, it's not. I get you're worried,
though. So, then, what did
you want to talk about?

"Grandma's an alcoholic."

Yeah, I kind of figured.

Cal's smart about stuff like that.
"You know it's a disease, right?"

He nods.

"And she can get treatment, right?"

Another nod.

"So, how do we convince her?"

We can't. Anyway, why
would I want to try?

"Because she's family, and
you could be one, too. Because
wouldn't you want someone
to try to convince you?"

FACT OR FICTION:
I Know a Lot About Addiction

Answer: More than any kid should.

I know

>what it was like to put a blanket
over my mom when she fell asleep
on the couch before dinner.

>The stuff she drank was brown,
not clear, but it smelled the same
on her breath as Grandma's.

>Some people say alcohol
can cause cancer. Which
came first? That's the question.

I know

>how it hurt to shrink back
into a corner when my dad
stormed in, eyes red and bulging.

>I was too little to understand
his nervous pacing and ranting
were symptoms of his drug use.

>But anyone could see him flip
from decent to dark-hearted.
The reason didn't matter then.

I know

> what it was like to go hungry,
> no money for food when a different
> hunger needed to be fed.

> There was never enough money.
> Dad would work. He'd get fired.
> Mom's waitress job didn't pay much.

> First Dad sold stuff. The Xbox
> I got for Christmas. His wedding ring.
> I'll never forget *that* argument!

I know

> how it felt to go to the school
> nurse because my teacher noticed
> a suspicious bruise on my arm.

> To have child protective services
> pay us a visit. To lie to the nice
> lady that I fell and hit a rock.

> To see the disbelief in her eyes.
> She'd heard the excuses before.
> But she left me there anyway.

I know

> what it meant when the cops
> came to the door, looking for Dad.
> They wanted to ask a few questions.

Was he home?
Where was he the night before?
Where was his weapon?

Turned out Dad's latest "job"
was using a gun to rob people.
The money he took all went for drugs.

Unfortunately, cameras caught him.
Fortunately, the judge was lenient.
That was still two years behind bars.

FACT OR FICTION:
I Confess All That to Hannah

Answer: I do not.

Because:
> It's none of her business.
> She wouldn't care anyway.

Instead, I tell Hannah,
"It's good you're worried,
but unless Grandma wants
help, she won't get it.
You can't change that."

> She sighs. *That's what
> Mom told me, too. So, we
> can't do anything?*

"My therapist says an
honest approach is best.
Tell Grandma you care
about her and are worried
she might be drinking too much."

> *What if she gets mad?*

"She probably will. But
at least you tried."

> *Will you tell her, too?*

"Hannah—"

At least go with me?

I agree that I will.

I mean, it's no big deal
to stand there while
Grandma lets her have it.

But I'm not quite ready
for more confrontation.
"Since we're already out,
let's actually ride for a bit."

Hannah says okay, and
we thread the neighborhood.
The streets are quiet,
which makes it nice,
and after a half hour or so,
we decide to head home.

Bad decision.

———

We are greeted with
a shouting match.

      Grandma
         versus
            Uncle Bruce.

It's ugly. And loud.

They're arguing about
him moving out.

Grandma: *How dare you?*

Uncle Bruce: *I don't answer to you!*

Grandma: *Answer to your wife, then!*

Uncle Bruce: *You stay out of this!*

Grandma: *Just another loser!*

Uncle Bruce: *I'm the loser? Me?*

Aunt Taryn tries to stop
them, but they circle around her.

The decibel level
is off the charts.
Every word,
every curse
is like a wrecking ball
against my skull.

My own voice is a roar.
"Quit! I can't take it!"

The sound turns off instantly.
Completely.
Until Grandma says,

This isn't about you.

FACT OR FICTION:
Enough Is Enough

Answer: We're way beyond enough.

I lower my voice, force
myself to keep it there.

"Nothing is about me
because I am nothing.

"I've never been anything
but somebody's problem.

"But you've got a problem,
too, Grandma. A big one."

I glance at Hannah, who's
watching, wide-eyed.

Is she going to step in
here? No? Okay, fine.

"Hannah and I"—*go ahead,
say it*—"are worried about you."

> Her head cocks. She's curious.
> *Worried about me? Why?*

I point to the glass in
her hand. "Because of that."

Oops. That wasn't supposed
to happen. Here we go.

"We think maybe you need
help. We want you to get it."

                      Her cheeks heat cranberry-red.
                      What do you know about it?

Less than an hour ago,
I thought about what I know.

"Want me to write it down
for you? It's a long list."

Grandma takes a couple
of very deep breaths.

Her shoulders relax a little.
She doesn't ask for the list.

                      Maybe I should just leave.
                      I can see I'm not appreciated.

Every one of us yells, "No!"
She definitely can't drive now.

                      Hannah jumps in. *We appreciate*
                      you, Grandma. We love you.

                      That's why we're worried.
                      We want you to stay alive.

FACT OR FICTION:
Hannah Went Too Far

Answer: Guess we'll find out.

The wrecking ball has quit
swinging. The room is silent.
It stays that way for ten
or fifteen very long seconds.

> Finally, Grandma says,
> *For your information, I don't*
> *plan to drop dead anytime*
> *soon. Thanks for caring, but*
> *everything's under control.*

At least she doesn't sound
mad, and we gave it a try.

Hannah looks like she wants
to say more. I shake my head
and she closes her mouth.
I think she just earned
some respect. If she pushes
too hard right now, she'll lose it.

> Aunt Taryn changes tactics.
> *Mom? I was thinking about*
> *turkey pot pie for dinner,*
> *and I've never managed*
> *to perfect your pie crust*
> *recipe. Would you help me?*

If you think I can manage
it in my condition, of course.

Everyone retreats.

    Aunt Taryn and Grandma
    to the kitchen. Before long,
    the clanks and clatters
    of bowls and baking pans
    tell a story without words.

        Uncle Bruce to his bedroom.
        He turns on some music,
        plays it loudly. Maybe
        trying to disguise the sound
        of packing a suitcase or two.

            Hannah to her own room.
            She says she'll be back
            in a while and maybe we'll
            find a movie. I can tell she's
            disappointed we didn't fix Grandma.

Grandma doesn't think
she's broken. Maybe not.
Maybe she's just chipped,
like an old plate with a piece
that's been missing too long.

You can picture how
it looked, imagine it all
shiny new and undamaged.
You know it will never be
exactly like that again.

I'm thinking about that
when the phone rings.

Once.
          Twice.
                    Three times.

Since no one else seems
like they're going to answer
it, I do. And wish I hadn't.

Cal? Is that you? You know
who this is, don't you, son?

Like I could ever forget
his voice. It gives me chills,
and I shiver. "Uh, hi, Dad."

So, I'm out of prison, and living
with Frank in Fresno.
That's not so far from you.

Not nearly far enough.
California's a big state,
but not big enough
to share it with him.

We've got a decent place,
a nice little trailer
just outside of the city . . .

I don't care.
I don't care.
I don't care.

He keeps talking and I hold
the phone away from my ear.

A noise like a million crickets
fires up inside my brain.

Duck.
Hide.
Run.

Aunt Taryn comes into
the living room, shoots me
her *is everything okay?* look.

I shake my head. "Hey, Dad?
I'm really happy here, and—"

*I know. I know. I just need
to see you, Cal. I plan
on making the trip down
sometime before Christmas.*

I don't hear anything else
he says, and I'm grateful
when I can tell him, "Goodbye."

FACT OR FICTION:
I Have No Idea What Dad Wants

Answer: Fact. Fact. Fact.

Why can't he just leave me alone?

There's already too much upset
in this house, and he'll only
make everything worse.

When I tell Aunt Taryn
about Dad's plan, she says,

> *I'll call our lawyer on Monday.*
> *But I'm not sure what we can do.*

"He can't take me away, right?"

> *Bruce and I are your legal*
> *guardians, so not without*
> *our permission, or a judge's.*

"I'm . . ." I should say
scared, but won't admit it.
So I finish with, "Worried."

She opens her arms, and I slump
into them. This is a real hug.
The kind my mom used to give me.

> *I will fight for you, Cal.*

Now I'm crying.

FACT OR FICTION:
Grandma and I Communicate Before She Leaves

Answer: Sort of.

It's not like we get one another
or will miss each other after she's gone.
But we do share one small moment
that may or may not mean something.

She's an early riser, like me.
Everyone else is still asleep
and I'm reading on the couch
when she wanders into the living room.

"Is something wrong?" I ask.

> *Not wrong, exactly. An owl*
> *woke me. He's right outside*
> *the bedroom window.*

"Yeah. He comes around
pretty often."

> *My papa used to say owls*
> *are messengers. Wonder what*
> *this one was trying to tell me.*

I picture a poster in Ms. C's
office. "Maybe that every day
brings a new beginning."

Definition of *Sea Change*:
Major Transformation

Grandma went home.
Dad moved out.
Mom got a part-time job,
working mornings at a daycare.
That means Cal and I have
to help around the house more.

We do laundry.
Wash the dishes.
Pack our lunch boxes.
Even dust and vacuum.

Mom says the last two weeks
have brought a sea change
to our lives, and she's right.

We're all so busy!
Christmas is coming,
and with it a dance recital
I'm madly rehearsing for.

Also, the school holiday play.
I'm only in the chorus,
but Cal has a talking part.
He's the lazy elf,
and he's got four whole lines,
which he can't remember.

Mrs. Peabody says not
to worry if he flubs them.
No one will know the difference.
I tell him practice makes perfect.

Dad won't make it
for the play, which is on
Thursday, but he swears
he'll be front and center
at the recital on Saturday.

Five whole days,
on top of the last fifteen!
I miss him so much.

It's not like three weeks
without him is so very long.
But what if next time it's
                    four?
                              five?
                                        six?

I left a letter for "Santa,"
who I quit believing in
when I was seven. But I hope
Mom will show it to Dad.
This is what it says:

Dear Kris Kringle,

I used to ask you to put lots
of things under the tree.

I don't even know if we'll have
a tree this year, but if we do,
don't worry about presents.

All I want for Christmas
is for Dad to move home.

                    Love, Hannah

Dad got a copy.
            He didn't say no.
                        But he didn't say okay.

Definition of *Agitated*:
Troubled; Nervous

One reason Cal's having a hard
time remembering his lines
is he's been kind of agitated.

I don't blame him.

Lately
we've noticed
a strange car
in the neighborhood,
and once when I looked
out the window
I saw it
cruise by
our house
super
slowly.

Two men
were inside.

One looked familiar.

When I told Mom,
she called the police.

They weren't
exactly helpful.

They said that wasn't a crime,
and even if it was Cal's dad
inside that car,
without a restraining order
(whatever that is)
they couldn't stop someone
from driving by.

Mom freaked out.

She went to her lawyer,
who informed Cal's dad
that Cal doesn't have to see him
unless a judge orders visitation.
They don't go to court until January.

A couple of days ago,
I heard Mom on the phone
with the lawyer.

> *The man wants money?*
> *How much? Seriously?*

I don't know how much,
but I figured out
Cal's dad would agree
to go away if he got paid.

That's so messed up.

I didn't tell Cal,
and I'm pretty sure
Mom didn't, either.

But she did tell
the lawyer,
                    We'll see him in court.

Definition of *Research*:
Gathering Information

Our last social studies
project before vacation
is to write about one
of the major holidays
that happen this time of year.

We can choose from
                    Hanukkah
                    Kwanzaa
                    Christmas
                    Boxing Day
                    Festivus

I've never heard of the last
one, so that's the one I pick.

We're just coming back
from lunch to start our research.
Mrs. Peabody takes
a head count and says,

                    Has anyone seen Cal?

I raise my hand. "He ate
in the media center.
He was helping
Mr. Gregg shelve books."

                    *Okay, well, we're a couple
                    of tablets short today.*

*Why don't you and Misty
and . . . Vic go to the media
center and start your research
on the computers there?
Cal, too. You have an hour.*

Why me? complains Vic.

*I've found it's best to separate
you and Bradley when there
are computers involved.
Have you picked your holiday?*

Vic rolls his eyes. *Boxing
Day. Duh. I like boxing.*

Mrs. Peabody smiles. *Yes,
well, I can see you have some
information to gather, so
you three run along.
Here's a hall pass for you.*

———

The media center was built
after the rest of our school.
Some old person who died
paid for it, and it's got
lots and lots of books,
plus a bank of computers.

It's at the end of a long
hallway and has lots
of windows, so you never
feel all closed in. It's rad.

Vic kind of dances behind
Misty and me, being his
usual annoying self.

> *Why are you guys in such
> a hurry?* he asks.

> *Because we only have
> an hour,* says Misty, who
> needs to research Kwanzaa.

> *Yeah, and . . . ?*

"Too late, Vic. We're here."
I can see Cal through
the glass, unloading books
from the return carts
onto the big stacks of shelves.

We go through the double
doors, clear the detectors.
"Hey, Cal. You're late for class."

His head jerks up toward
the clock on the wall.
*Oh, man. I wasn't paying
attention to the time.*

> *Mrs. Peabody said you can
> do detention here,* teases Vic.

At least he's not playing bully.
Still, I hurry to correct, "Not
really. She sent us to research
our reports and said for you
to work here, too. You're cool."

> *Where's Mr. Gregg?* asks Misty.

> *He went down to the office
> for a couple of minutes.
> He'll be right back.*

"Can we go ahead and use
the computers?"

> *Sure,* says Cal. *I can sign us—*

Three short bursts of the fire
alarm interrupt, followed by

Hard lockdown; hard lockdown; hard lockdown.

Definition of *Panic*:
What Happens Next

No. No way.
Three "hard lockdowns"
mean this is not a drill.

We've done those
lots of times.
But this is different.

Teachers, lock your doors and follow protocol.

Huge problem.
Too many windows.
No place to hide.

> *Quick!* urges Misty.
> *What do we do?*

Can't make it to a classroom.
Can't go out in the hall.

People running.
Screaming.
Doors slamming.

> Cal grasps my hand.
> *I know! Come on!*

We sprint to a storage
room in an office behind
the librarian's desk.

Grab the biggest books
you can find in case
we have to throw them.

Once we're all inside,
he locks the door and
turns off the light.

We huddle together
against the far wall.

I'm shaking so hard,
it rattles the pictures
on the wall
above our heads.

Misty knots her fingers
into mine. *I can't breathe.*

Don't panic, says Cal.
Do what I do. He sucks
in air. Holds it. Releases.

We all do our best
to copy him. But I
can barely manage.

My racing heart thumps
so loudly, I'm afraid
it will give us away.

"I'm scared," I moan.

>   *Me too*, murmurs Vic.
>   *I don't want to die.*

> *Stop it*, orders Cal.
> *We're not going to die.*

He lowers his voice
to barely a whisper.

This reminds me of
the time I got locked
in a closet for three days.
Did I ever tell you
that story, Hannah?

Definition of *Distraction*:
Something That Takes Your Mind Off Things

Like Cal's whispered story:

> *After Mom died, I moved*
> *in with a roaming band*
> *of carnies. We caravaned*
> *around the country, setting*
> *up rides and games*
> *at rodeos and carnivals.*
>
> *Mostly, we lived in the vans,*
> *but every once in a while,*
> *if we made enough money,*
> *we'd crash in motel rooms*
> *for a night or two . . .*
>
> *Being the newest member*
> *of the outfit, sometimes*
> *they forgot I was with them.*
> *Anyway, this one time*
> *I sneaked into the motel-*
> *room closet to see how much*
> *money we had socked away.*
>
> *I don't know how the door*
> *got locked, but it did. At first,*
> *I didn't want to pound on it*
> *because I'd get caught.*
> *But then I had to . . . you know,*
> *go, so I started yelling.*

No one came for three days.
Which means, yeah, I had to
go in the closet. It was gross
when the motel manager
finally came around.

> *Sure*, says Vic. *So, what*
> *happened to the carnies?*

I sigh. "Vic, Cal never lived with
any carnies."

> *Shush*, whispers Misty.
> *Don't make so much noise.*

We all stop talking.
Stop moving.
Listen.
Nothing.
"Maybe it was a false
alarm," I whisper.

> *We have to stay put until*
> *we hear the all clear*, says Cal.

> *What if it doesn't come?*
> Misty sobs. *What if—*

> *Yeah*, interrupts Vic.
> *What if we suffocate?*

That's not going to happen.

                       How do you know?

Cal is quiet for a moment.
*I really did get locked in
a closet for three days.
Well, two and a half.
But not by the carnies.*

By my dad.

*I lived with him after Mom died.
At first it was okay.
He had a job and a decent
apartment. Then his brother
got out of prison and moved in.*

*Uncle Frank used drugs.
Pretty soon, so did Dad.
Sometimes they went on
benders—long drug parties.*

*They were having one
of those and didn't want
a kid around, so they locked
me in the closet. Gave me
a bucket to use for a toilet.*

I ate peanuts. Jerky. Water.
To keep me quiet, they gave
me cold medicine, which
made me really sleepy.

You never told anyone?
asks Misty.

I was afraid they'd take me
away. Even a bad parent
seemed better than none.
But then Dad was arrested
and Uncle Frank got kicked
out of the apartment.

He and I lived on the street.
He made me steal food
and hustle money. You know,
make sad eyes at nice ladies
so they'd give me a few bucks.

Why didn't you just tell
him no? asks Vic.

Did you ever get the belt?

Oh, yeah. More than once.

FACT OR FICTION:
Vic and I Have Something in Common

Answer: Yes, and it doesn't surprise me.

No time to think about that now.
There is noise outside the door.

At least one person is moving
loudly through the library.

I've tried to keep everyone
distracted, but now it's impossible.

I hold up one hand, and they
all understand it means silence.

Footsteps. Heavy. Tables, chairs
scooting. At last, a deep voice:

                                              Anyone in here?

There's been no all clear.
I put a finger to my lips.

                                              This is the police.

Hannah starts to move.
I stop her. "We don't know."

Slap-slap-slap. Pacing closer.
We all hold on to each other.

Pick up our books, get ready
to throw them if it comes to that.

The door handle rattles.
Hannah whimpers.

I move in front of her.
Vic does the same for Misty.

We look at each other, nod.
If someone comes through . . .

Now there's another voice.
And this one we know.

Let me. They'll be scared.
Kids? You're safe now.

"Mrs. Peabody? Is that you?"
Wait. "You're not being coerced?"

Yes, Calvin Pace, it's me,
Mrs. Peabody. I'm here with
Officers Ash and Kraft.

Okay, she knows my name,
and it sounds like her.

Still, I stay in front of the girls.
"Vic? Open up. But be ready."

He stands cautiously, walks
to the door, steps to one side.

Hannah is shaking. Misty moves
closer. "Okay. Now." I lift my book . . .

It's really Mrs. Peabody. Hannah
and Misty jump up and run to her.

> Come on. We need to go. You
> can put down the books, boys.

I can see respect in her eyes.
I think we did good.

FACT OR FICTION:
We Made It

Answer: We did.

We were lucky. Or smart.
Or both. Definitely both.

The cops look pretty nervous
as they escort us through a back exit.
Outside, the school is surrounded
by police cars and ambulances.
I can see two stretchers being loaded.

"What happened?" I ask.

> *We're still gathering the facts,*
> says Officer Ash. *Let's go.*
> *We have a rendezvous*
> *location set up where your*
> *parents can come get you.*

The four of us kids hold hands
as we follow her around
the building and across the street
and down the block to a church.

Mrs. Peabody walks behind us.
She rests a hand on my shoulder,
and I ask, "Were we the last ones out?"

*Yes. The media center is at the far
end of the building. That's why
there wasn't an all clear. They had
to be sure there were no other intruders.*

We were so scared! says Misty.

I know, says Mrs. Peabody.
But you did exactly the right thing.

Thanks to Cal, says Vic. *We freaked,
but he knew what to do.*

That makes me feel good.
And now Mrs. Peabody
squeezes my arm.

I'm glad you were there.

Officer Ash turns and looks
me in the eye. *Good job.*

Inside the church, people cry
and hug, and whatever relief
they must feel is swallowed up,
knowing how close they came
to losing each other.

Officer Ash walks us over
to the big table where they're
checking off names and matching
kids with their parents.

> *Okay. I've got to get back.*
> *I'm glad you're all safe.*

Misty's mom spots her right
away and runs over to hold her.

> Vic looks around. *I don't see*
> *my parents. Dad's probably*
> *out on a job. Can I call my mom?*

Mrs. Peabody hands him
her phone and asks Hannah,

> *Do you see your parents?*

We start to say no, but
just as we do, Aunt Taryn
rushes in. I point. "There."

> She reaches us in seconds
> flat, out of breath and words.
> *Oh. Oh.* Her hug is massive.

Mrs. Peabody tells her,
*You should be very proud
of the kids. Especially Cal.
I hear he took charge when
he needed to. Thank you, Cal.*

It takes a few minutes
for Aunt Taryn to collect us
and take us home. By the time
we reach the car, we're all crying.

*I'm sorry it took me so long,
but I couldn't leave the daycare
until I could call someone in.*

                    Did you tell Dad? asks Hannah.

Yes. He's on his way.

"Do you know what happened?"

*Not all the details. There
was an armed intruder.
The police were there fast,
though. And no kids were hurt.*

FACT OR FICTION:
Uncle Bruce Makes a Two-Hour Drive in an Hour and a Half

Answer: That's what he claims.

I don't know if it's true
or not, but we're barely home
when he comes skidding up.

He jumps out of his car
like it's on fire, and barrels
toward us. It isn't just Hannah
he pulls into his arms.

It feels weird.
And good.

> *You're okay. You're okay.*
> He keeps repeating it,
> over and over. *You're okay.*

Finally, he lets us go,
then he gives Aunt Taryn
a giant kiss, and I don't
remember seeing him
smooch her like that before.

We all go inside and Uncle
Bruce asks us about how
we hid in the closet.

For once, I let Hannah
tell the story.

FACT OR FICTION:
I Was Right to Worry About Dad

Answer: I should have worried more.

I worried he'd show up.
>   He did.

I worried he'd cause trouble.
>   He did.

I didn't worry about him
trying to take me from school.
>   He did. With Uncle Frank.

It took a few days, but finally
we got all the ugly details.

When Dad and Uncle Frank went
into the office, our secretary, Mrs. Lopez,
refused to tell them where I was.

Dad insisted he had the right
to pick up his son.
Mrs. Lopez disagreed.

Dad started toward the hallway.
Mrs. Lopez yelled for him to stop.

Uncle Frank pulled a gun.
Mrs. Lopez screamed, *Firearm!*

Mr. Love initiated the lockdown.

Ms. Crowell came running.
So did the school security guard.

Officer Pete tackled Uncle Frank.
The gun went off and a bullet
hit Ms. C in the shoulder.

Officer Pete is a pretty big guy.
He squashed Uncle Frank,
damaged a couple of his ribs.

Dad tried to run, but by the time
he hit the front door, patrol cars
were screeching into the parking lot.

Kidnap fail.

That story must sound
like I made it up. I didn't.

I told it like that—
start to finish, with nothing
extra added—
because emotions
are jumbled inside my head.

I feel:

Relieved.	It could've been worse.
Sorry.	Ms. C got hurt.
Guilty.	It was my dad.
Thankful.	He's back in prison.
Uneasy.	I'm thankful about that.

My father will be behind bars
for a very long time.
That makes me feel safe.

Also, sad.
I wish I had a better dad.

Definition of *Hero*:
The Person Who Saves the Day

It's Christmas Eve.
We have a tree.
With presents under it.

Cal is in his room,
wrapping something.

Dad and Mom are sipping
eggnog. I would, but I hate it.
Adults are weird.

I don't know for sure
if Kris Kringle granted my wish,
but Dad has been home
since the lockdown.
Eleven days.

He and Mom haven't argued
even one time.

That's a good sign.

Pretty soon, we're all going
to watch *It's a Wonderful Life*.
I've seen it before, but that's
okay. It's a rad movie.

On the news tonight,
they said Ms. C is going
to be all right, and back
at work after vacation.

They also said she pushed
in between Cal's uncle
and Mrs. Lopez, knowing
she might get shot.

She's a real hero.

After I heard that,
I thought about how Cal
moved in front of me
when we were in the closet.

He's kind of a hero, too.
Not that I'd tell him that.

> *Cal!* calls Mom. *The movie
> starts in five minutes.*

> *Coming!*

He appears,
carrying a present,
which he offers to me.

"You want me to open it
now? Or wait till tomorrow?"

      Now.

His eyes shine
with excitement.

      I had to order it special.

I untie the red ribbon,
carefully remove the tape
from the gold foil wrapping paper.

Open it s-l-o-w-l-y,
smiling at Cal's impatience.

And inside is . . .

      a sparkly purple competition leotard.

Definition of *Epilogue*:
The Conclusion of a Book

I'm Hannah Lincoln,
and one day I'll qualify
for the Olympics.

Or I'll be a dancer.
Or an actress.
Or, who knows?

Maybe I'll be the first
astronaut to touch
down on Mars.

Or maybe all four.

                    Why not try to touch the sky?

My cousin, Calvin Pace,
still drives me crazy.

He still has meltdowns,
though not as often
as he used to.

He still plays
stupid pranks.
Mostly, they're funny.

And he still makes up
outrageous stories.

He's still a fake kid.

But I guess if you plan on
writing fiction,

that's not such a bad thing to be.

FACT OR FICTION:
I'm Not Lost Anymore

Answer: Mostly true.

I'm Cal, and I still feel a little lost
when I think about my mom.
I guess I always will.

But things are better now.

Uncle Bruce decided to move
back, which made Aunt Taryn
and Hannah so happy.
Not only that, but he told me,

>   *I'm sorry if I haven't always*
>   *made you feel welcome here.*
>   *But I want you to know*
>   *that you are an important*
>   *part of this family. I hope*
>   *we can become close.*

We agreed to work on that.
And then we watched a game.

I still lose it sometimes
and I still have nightmares.

But I also have good dreams.
And I remember them.

I called Grandma on her birthday.
Pretty sure that made her cry.
Hannah and I argue,
and I'll probably always prank her.
Just not in a mean way.

That home in the distance,
the one I could never reach?
Today, I'm much closer to it
than I am to nowhere.

AUTHOR'S NOTE

My first young-adult novel, *Crank*, was inspired by the very true story of my daughter's walk with the monster substance crystal meth. Our family has fought this addiction with her for twenty-four years, watching her thrive during periods of sobriety only to fall again through relapse. Though she seems to be stable now, we live with the fear of her stumbling again.

In that span of time, she has given birth to seven children. All have different fathers. My husband and I adopted the first, who is now twenty-three years old. The next two live separately with their paternal aunts. Six years ago, during an extremely brutal relapse, my daughter left her young children, ages three, four, and nine, with the brother of her boyfriend at the time. We found them living in squalor and took custody of the three.

The oldest came to us with severe emotional problems, the result of early childhood trauma suffered at the hands of one or more of the men who'd been ushered through his life. At the time, he had daily breakdowns at home, in school, and in public spaces. Whenever too much came at him—noise, expectation, rules, bullying—he'd throw himself on the floor or pull into a corner and scream. PTSD was the diagnosis.

That was the reputation he developed in fourth grade, and it has followed him all the way to high school, where he's a sophomore as I write this. Years of therapy and counseling have mitigated the behaviors. The breakdowns still happen, but they are rare. Months apart. He does take off sometimes as a way of dealing with too much pressure. (He's always home before dark.) In his mind, rules tend to be optional, losing impossible. Playing games with him isn't always fun. And rather than admit mistakes, the boy makes up stories. Whoppers.

But he has a huge heart, something most people never see because they won't give him second or third chances to reveal his positive traits. He has a genius-level IQ and excels at math, science, and technology. He also loves to cook and read and ski. He's kind to animals. Still, six years of working hard to get better haven't netted him many friends. As an aside, raising a difficult child affects every family member, especially when the parent figures don't agree on the best way to handle the outbursts. My marriage has survived, but there have been times I doubted it would.

Cal in this book is very much inspired by our brilliant, weird, wonderful child. Their stories are different, though their person-alities are similar. I hope this book will plant seeds of empathy for kids with behavioral problems they can't always control. They don't want to be classroom "freaks." They want friends. They want to fit in, even when it's difficult to tamp down their emotions. They deserve a deeper look and another chance. And another. And another.

ACKNOWLEDGMENTS

With love and gratitude to my own unique children, both grown and growing into adulthood. Each of you has also faced unique challenges and gifted me with your presence in my life. A huge nod here to my husband, who has weathered every storm and remained the cornerstone of our family. With special thanks to my editor, Stacey Barney, and every member of the Penguin team, who have welcomed me and helped make this book one I take great pride in. I'm certain it will make a positive difference in many young lives and can't wait to see it in readers' hands. One last shout-out to all the amazing teachers and librarians charged with building the future through the kids whose lives they help model. Y'all rock!